HiddenScars

Hidden Scars

A Novel By

Michelle A. Marsh

DEDICATION

This book is dedicated in memory of my mother,
Lela Mae (Bester) Bender,
my angel, who loved me unconditionally.

As well as those who continue to push past their pain,
to heal their "Hidden Scars."

PRELUDE

"Push Grace, push!"

I screamed to the heavens.

"Stay focused. You got this."

I thought, only heaven could help now.

"Okay, breathe," Macie said, as she coached me.

I slowly inhaled through my nose and slowly breathed out of my mouth.

The palpitations were so fast, I could feel my heart beating in my throat.

Tears were flowing down my face. The pain that I felt, was raw.

The fear of the unknown was real.

The scars were no longer hidden.

"You're doing good Grace. You're almost at the finish line."

I squeezed Macie's hand as tight as I could as if I was transferring the pain. She grimaced, not uttering a word, understanding my agony.

"Give me one more big push Grace. I see his head crowning. Give it all you got," Dr. Freelance said.

"Uhhhgggggg!" I pushed past the pain, with everything inside of me.

With all of the feelings of anger and hurt, that I had built up, beyond the huge betrayal. Truth is, I wanted it all out of me, just as much as my son. I pushed and pushed until I heard my baby boy let out a loud cry.

"You did it! Good job Grace!" Macie exclaimed. "Now keep breathing," she said, massaging her sore hand.

I rested my head on the pillow, looking up at the white ceiling, as I continued to take small breaths.

"I'm so proud of you!" Macie said as she fed me a few ice chips.

After my baby boy was all cleaned up, Dr. Freelance laid him on top of my chest.

My emotions were numb.

"Congratulations Grace! You have given birth to a healthy baby boy, born at 7:32 p.m. and weighing in at six pounds and four ounces," Dr. Freelance said.

"It's finally over," he said.

Is it really over? I thought. Or had it only just begun?

In my heart, I knew that this was only the beginning.

This was one of the many days to come that would change our lives forever.

I looked at my son, as I lifted up the blanket that he was wrapped in, counting his ten fingers and ten toes. I saw a small image of me inside of my baby's little face.

"Have you thought of a name for your beautiful baby boy?" Dr. Freelance asked, rolling back on the stool, as he pulled off the bloody latex gloves.

"Yes," I replied.

"His name is, Justice."

CHAPTER 1

Knock, Knock, Knock!

"Who goes there?" Old Man Joe said talking through the closed door.

"Old Man Joe, it's Grace. Momma sent me to get the rent."

"Tell your momma that the check is in the mail and stop bothering me."

I had a puzzled look on my face.

"We live right upstairs. Why would you mail the rent when you know that the first of the month is today?" I asked, placing my ear close to the door, waiting for his response.

"Gal, you better put some respect on my name and stop questioning me," he said as if my question was not valid.

"That doesn't make any sense to me," I said.

"I'm gonna knock some sense into you if you don't get away from my door," he said.

"It'll reach her before the 15th. Even credit card companies give you a grace period. Besides, if it wasn't for me, your momma would probably still be living in them projects, feeding you kids government cheese," he said.

"Now, shoo and get away from my door gal," he wailed banging his cane on the door, attempting to scare me away.

I jumped back, startled by the loud noise.

"Old Man Joe," I said hearing his heavy breathing through the door.

"Gal, you are as annoying as a fly at a barbecue," he said, "Now what?"

"Momma, sent you down a bowl of banana pudding," I said, placing the bowl, wrapped in foil, in front of the door.

As I walked toward the steps, I peeked around the corner, to see that Old Man Joe had opened the door, and guided the bowl into the house, with his cane and slammed the door shut!

Old Man Joe may have been seventy-one but he was a feisty little old man. Momma said that she and her childhood best friend Ms. Purlie met him thirty years ago when she sold her catfish dinners down at the dance hall.

Old Man Joe was known to be a player, always looking casket sharp and courting ladies twenty years his junior. Sometimes more than one at a time. When a few of them popped up pregnant, he dipped into his 401k, taking hardship withdrawals from his retirement fund, using it like hush money, paying for whatever they or the kids needed, until his funds ran out. Some of them were too embarrassed to even admit that they got knocked up by him.

If there was one thing that he could not resist about Momma, it was her cooking. He'd fallen in love with Momma's cooking, so much so, that when the head cook position at his job became available, he used his clout as supervisor, to get Momma the job.

That's where Momma met our Daddy. Momma proved that the best way to a man's heart is through his stomach. Momma told us that Daddy was smitten, after eating her fried chicken, macaroni and cheese, breaded fried okra, collard greens, with smoked turkey necks and buttered cornbread.

After Daddy tasted Momma's peach cobbler and her red velvet cake, Momma said that one day Daddy surprised her. He used the money that he was saving to buy a 1987 Cadillac and bought her a diamond ring instead. Daddy proposed and married Momma in less than a year of meeting her. It didn't take Daddy long before he had Momma barefoot and pregnant. Next thing you know, they had a house full of kids.

I enjoyed listening to Momma talk about Daddy because unlike my siblings, I didn't get a chance to know my Daddy, although Momma said that I looked spitting image of him.

Right before my first birthday, my Daddy was taken away from us. He was murdered by a cop who mistook him for a robbery suspect. Once we were old enough to understand, Momma told us that Daddy walked out of the gas station, minding his own business, with his change in one hand and his cigarettes in the other, when the cop shot Daddy in the chest, killing him instantly and leaving Momma to raise four kids by herself.

Momma wanted something good to come out of Daddy's death, so that's when she invested in the two-family apartment building that we live in, with the money that the town, where Daddy was murdered in, awarded her for Daddy's wrongful death.

After Daddy's death, Old Man Joe lost everything that he had ever owned, except the clothes off of his back, after the women that he was sleeping with found out about each other. They had him in court so much that the court security officers would address him by name. The women, just as they had been in his life, were like a revolving door, in and out of the courthouse, some with their children in tow, proving that "he was the daddy." Right after that, his senility kicked in and forced him into retirement with nowhere to go.

Momma felt that she was indebted to him, for getting her the job that allowed her to meet Daddy, and didn't think twice about renting the first-floor apartment out to him.

That's why Momma never put up much of a fuss when Old Man Joe paid his rent late. Besides, Section 8 paid the bulk of it. Momma said, we'd probably be homeless if we had to depend on the $120.00 that Old Man Joe was responsible for paying!

CHAPTER 2

If the pain of losing Daddy wasn't enough, watching Momma on the day that she lost her best friend, was just so unbearable to watch. It hurt like a head full of tight hair extensions, that no amount of Tylenol could relieve.

Momma talked about Ms. Purlie so much, that she seemed like an imaginary person since us kids couldn't remember meeting her.

But unlike when she spoke about Daddy, talking about Ms. Purlie always took Momma to a place of pain.

Momma said that they were once, thick as thieves but Ms. Purlie had vanished, not even calling Momma on her birthday or holidays. All Momma's calls to Ms. Purlie went straight to voicemail, so Momma just stopped calling. Then, one day, when Momma least expected it, while she was in the kitchen making some pecan pies to take to the dance hall, the phone rang. Although I had never met her, I knew that it was Ms. Purlie on the other end by the excitement Momma showed. That's when I realized, that she was a real, live person and it wasn't just a figment of my imagination. But Momma's excitement quickly turned to anger.

I overheard Momma talking to Ms. Purlie, saying, "If he asks, what do you want me to tell him Purlie? I will not lie for you. The truth will set you free."

Whatever Ms. Purlie was saying on the other end, agitated Momma so bad, that she started yelling at Ms. Purlie saying, "I'm tired of bailing you out of your sinful situations, Purlie!"

I was too young to figure out what Momma meant, but whatever Ms. Purlie had done, angered Momma. Before Momma got off of the phone with Ms. Purlie, she called her an, "irresponsible, low down dirty hoochie," and slammed the phone down. I asked Momma what was a hoochie but Momma gave me the look of death. So, I knew right then and there, that it was something bad. I don't know what could have made Momma so upset but that was the last Momma heard from Ms. Purlie, that I knew of.

Whatever was said that day, weighed Momma down like an anchor. It was as if, she was carrying a burden that needed lifting. It became clear that Momma didn't want any reminder of Ms. Purlie when she abruptly stopped selling her food at the dance hall and started a soup kitchen down at the church.

Momma had us in church, practically every day. She told us that we all needed a little more Jesus, but I knew better. Whatever change that had come over Momma, had Ms. Purlie's name written all over it. Momma did everything she could to block her out of her mind. Momma played Shirley Caesar's eight track tape, "Let Jesus Fix It," so much, that it started to repeat right at the part that said, "He knows." Something came over Momma. She pulled the magnetic tape out and tossed it and the cartridge right in the trash! If that wasn't enough, Momma unplugged the Panasonic 8 track stereo player, slapped a sign on it that read, "FREE!" and sat it on the sidewalk, replacing it with a three-speed turntable, cassette deck, and a CD disk player.

Just when we thought that Jesus had fixed it, Momma started taking us down to the church for 5:30 am prayer, before school, evening prayer, after school and if that wasn't enough, she made sure that we all had a prayer partner. We spent more time on our knees and in the church in a week than we did at home and school combined. That may be a stretch of the truth, but in my young mind, that's how it felt. But once Momma was diagnosed with leukemia, she stopped going to church on a regular basis and so did we. But if Momma taught us one thing, she taught us how to pray without ceasing.

As for Ms. Purlie, Momma never so much as hummed her name after that!

CHAPTER 3

Franklin was the oldest of the four of us. He was tall, dark, and very handsome. He owned any room that he entered. He stood 6'1" and had a muscular frame liken to "the Rock." His short wavy hair would make any woman sea sick. He had a way of driving all of the ladies crazy, with his good looks and baritone voice.

Franklin joined the military right after high school because he knew that college was too expensive for Momma to pay for, even with the extra money that she received from renting out to Old Man Joe.

Even though Franklin was stationed two hours away, he didn't come see Momma as much as she would have wanted him too. Part of the reason why his visits were so infrequent, is that Momma put him to work as soon as he walked through the door since she couldn't rely on David to do anything that required manual labor. We all knew that Franklin held a special place in Momma's heart. After Daddy died, he took on the responsibility of being the man of the house. He would even help out our elderly neighbors, doing small jobs for them, like taking out their trash or running errands to the corner store.

Growing up, I looked up to Franklin, like he was my hero. Mainly because he spent a lot of time coming to my rescue, like Superman. He would come to my defense, any time our other siblings would mistreat me or would bully me. I'll admit, at times I could be bratty like Dee from "What's Happening," but just like her brother Raj, Franklin was always so forgiving.

We were so close, that when he turned eighteen, he got a job driving an ice cream truck. He would let me go to work with him, as long as my homework was done. I would help him sell ice cream, like I was his little assistant. He didn't pay me but he would let me eat whatever I wanted, which meant all of the orange cream bars, until the day we discovered that I was lactose intolerant. When Momma went off to work, Franklin and I would go through her old records. I would put on Momma's Chaka Kahn wig and me and Franklin would lip sync to Ashford and Simpson's song "Solid," which for us, represented the close brother and sister bond that we shared. Franklin would hold the microphone, as we both swayed side to side to the beat of the music.

On the day that Franklin left for the military, I felt as if I was losing my best friend. I cried so hard, as I held onto his leg and begged him to take me with him, as his little sister soldier. That's when Franklin bent down, wiped my tears away and he promised me, that he would be back. I believed him.

CHAPTER 4

Now my oldest sister Anna Mae, she was a different story. Anna Mae was two years younger than Franklin. On her eighteen birthday, she surprised all of us, when she packed up and moved in with her boyfriend Rufus, escaping Momma's strict rules. She never looked back.

A short time after that, she and Rufus eloped, stripping Momma of the opportunity to be the proud mother of the bride. Anna Mae told Momma that she was abiding by the good book that says, "It's better to marry, than to burn." But I knew the truth. Truth was, Anna Mae just wanted to have wild passionate sex, just like she read in those magazines that she hid under her mattress, along with them edible underwear and those fruit flavored condoms.

But Momma sure did prep her to be wifey material. When Anna Mae was eleven, Momma kept her right by her side in the kitchen, grooming her, like she was going to be the next Rachel Ray.

By the time Anna Mae was thirteen, she knew how to cook just as good as Momma. Any time I came into the kitchen to help, she would tell Momma that I was in the way. She wanted to make sure that the only thing I mastered, was opening up a can of Pork and Beans!

When Momma wasn't around, Anna Mae would throw her weight around, giving us a time limit to come and eat, treating us like we were pigs eating out of a trough. God forbid if we didn't hear her calling for us to come eat, she would shut the kitchen down like Fort Knox and pack up all the food, using her body as a barricade between us and the refrigerator.

Anna Mae and I had a pretty decent relationship up until I hit my teenage years and started filling out in all the right places. It was then, that she started treating me more like a foe, than family. It came to the point, where I stopped being sad about the way that Anna Mae treated me and I just simply got used to her treating me like dog poop.

The turning point in our relationship came when I realized that I could not trust Anna Mae. She made it her mission to ridicule me in front of anyone and everyone. Spilling every secret that I'd ever told her as if it were a can of pinto beans. She was always willing to throw some shade my way. Over time I learned that the only thing that I could share with her was the table that Momma made us sit down at, for Sunday dinner.

CHAPTER 5

Twenty-one-year-old David was cute in the face but plump in the waist. He stood 5'9" and weighed 220lbs. He sported a short afro and a shabby beard. His barbed wire tattoo, that he got at seventeen, against Momma's will, looked more like stretched rubber bands, from all of the weight he'd gained. Out of all of us, David was the most irresponsible. Simply put, he was lazy! He could not hold a job and depended on Momma more than those Depend underwear, that we saw on the television commercials.

Momma always said, all of the gray hairs on her head had David's name written all over it. The older he got, the more he challenged Momma and her rules. If Momma asked him to do something, he would raise his voice, trying to instill fear in her, talking back, like he'd lost his ever-loving mind. But David was smart enough to not push his luck with Momma when Franklin was around. He knew that Franklin would have jacked him up!

By the time he turned eighteen, he just had a bad attitude all the way around. It seemed as if he was angry at the world. When Momma started allowing him to hang out with his friends, thinking it would change his mood, it only went from bad to worse.

He started sneaking out at night, then coming in at all hours of the morning, reeking like alcohol. Once Momma's health started to fail, she just didn't have the strength to discipline David. He took advantage of that and did whatever he wanted.

As for my relationship with David, we got along like oil and water. Besides being lazy, he was an overgrown bully. He would fist-fight me over everything, including food. One time, he nearly broke my arm in two places after I reached into the kitchen cabinet for the last Funny Bone snack cake that Momma use to buy us, as a treat. He'd shoved me so hard into the refrigerator, that I ended up in an arm splint for three weeks. At 5'1" and 110 pounds soaking wet, I was clearly no match for him!

CHAPTER 6

David and I were the only two still living at home. At nineteen, I took a paid leave of absence from my job to tend to Momma. The leukemia had crippled her so bad, that she needed care around the clock. The visiting nurses would come once a week to do her laundry but for the most part, all of the responsibility to care for Momma fell on me.

Unless I bribed David with some food, getting him to help was nearly impossible. I don't know if he was mad because he didn't get a big birthday party celebration, like Momma threw Franklin and Anna Mae when they turned twenty-one. Or, that most of his friends, had parents who could afford to buy them their first car, even if it was a hooptie. David either used Momma's car, usually against her will, took a bus or used those size ten feet that he had, walking to wherever the meet up spot was. David just refused to understand that Momma wasn't nearly the person, she was a few years ago, especially on this one particular Saturday morning in July.

I remember this morning like no other. I woke up in the mood to cook, as the bright sun peeked through my blinds and kissed my face. I had gotten up, washed my face brushed my teeth and made way into the kitchen to make me, Momma and David some banana pancakes. I knew they weren't going to taste as good as Momma or Anna Mae's but I did my best to follow the instructions in the cookbook to the T.

Momma had rung her bell, which meant she needed help getting into the bathroom.

"David, Grace, hurry up now before I have an accident!" she exclaimed.

The leukemia had attacked Momma's bones and joints, making it difficult for her to even walk short distances, with no assistance. Momma depended heavily on me and David to help her get around the house. I marched into David's room with the spatula in my hand and waved it over his crusty eyes.

"David, you hear Momma ringing the bell," I said. "Get your lazy behind up and go help her! You can smell that I am cooking!"

"Grace, if you don't stop waving that thing in my face, I'm going to stick it up your butt," he said as he rolled off of the edge of the bed, wiping his eyes, and yawning with his mouth wide open as if he was catching flies.

David walked past me, shoving me in the shoulder, making me lose my balance. I watched him as he walked toward Momma's room.

"I'm in control like Janet Jackson. You better do what I say" I said, under my breath, as I giggled to myself.

As I walked back into the kitchen, all of a sudden, I heard a big bang and Momma yelp. Immediately, I dropped the spatula and I rushed toward the bathroom where Momma was. As I stood in the door way, there she lay on the floor with blood gushing out of the back of her head. David stood motionless staring down at Momma. He was in just as much shock, as I felt.

"What happened!" I screamed at David, as I ran over kneeling down next to Momma.

"I don't know, she was standing at the sink, and just lost her balance. She fell back and banged her head on the tub," David said.

"Momma are you okay!" I shouted.

Momma's eyes started to roll to the back of her head. She was unresponsive.

"Don't move her!" I said, as I looked toward Momma's side table, where the telephone was. Blood started running profusely from the huge gash on the back of Momma's head.

"David, we have to get Momma help, before she bleeds to death," I said. I ran to the telephone in Momma's room, stretching the long chord into the bathroom, near Momma's head and started dialing 911.

"Momma, are you okay. Talk to me," I said as the phone rang.

A woman came on the phone.

"911. What's your emergency?" she said.

"I need an ambulance right away to 46 Rosehill Way. My Momma had a hard fall and she's bleeding to death!" I screamed.

"Ma'am calm down. Where is she now," the woman asked. I could hear her typing.

"She's in the bathroom with me and my brother. He said she fell back and hit her head on the tub," I said.

I could see Momma going in and out of consciousness.

"David talk to her!" I screamed.

"Calm down. Stay with me," the woman said. "Do not move her. Keep her head still," the woman continued, doing her best to try and calm me down. I was in complete hysterics, as tears started to roll down my cheeks.

"Okay. An ambulance is on the way. Try to keep her awake and continue talking to her until the paramedics arrive," the woman instructed.

"Okay, okay," I said.

I held the phone for comfort. The woman on the other end sounded cool as a cucumber. I was anything but! Fear had gripped my body watching Momma lay there so still. Every second that passed felt like an eternity. It wasn't long before the loud sound of sirens crept its way up our dead end street. The closer they got to our house, the tighter fear gripped my heart.

"I hear them outside," I said abruptly and hung up the phone.

CHAPTER 7

I sat in the emergency room at the hospital still in shock, as David and I waited to get a second update on Momma. The doctor came out earlier and told us, what I had dreaded hearing. Momma's hard fall had been worse than we'd thought and that she fell into a coma on the way to the hospital. Hearing what happened to Momma, knowing that she was alone in the back of the ambulance, angered me. I had asked David to ride with Momma and I would follow in Momma's car behind them, but he wouldn't. He seemed more upset that I wouldn't give him the keys to Momma's car, refusing to let him drive on a suspended license.

As I faced the entrance of the emergency room, I saw Rufus pull up in front of the double doors, in his silver Mercedes Benz. The sun shined through the open sun roof, hitting his jerry curl, as it sparkled like new money.

Anna Mae stepped out of the car and sauntered her way toward the entrance of the hospital emergency doors.

We hadn't seen Anna Mae in over a year. She was dressed like she was going to a cocktail party. She had on a black Marc Jacobs balloon sleeve dress, with yellow polka dots and black patent leather Louis Vuitton red bottom shoes, with a matching Louis Vuitton black purse, that dangled from her arm.

Anna Mae was what you would call "fancy." Her hair was done, her nails were done, everything overdone, including the MAC makeup that was caked on her high cheekbones. She had replaced her thick coke bottle glasses for hazel contact lenses that blended well with her coffee colored skin. She stood 5'8" and was thick, just like a milkshake. Her double D breasts complimented her full thighs and size twenty-nine-inch waistline but her butt, now that was a different story. It screamed "Caution, wide load," and was flat as a penny!

"Ma'am can I help you," the ER secretary asked Anna Mae as she continued walking by, as if she didn't see the woman or the rather large sign that read, "All visitors must sign in."

Anna Mae stopped dead in her tracks and turned toward the secretary, looking over her Gucci shades, "Do I look like I need help?"

The secretary pointed to the sign and said in a sarcastic and loud voice, "ALL VISITORS, that means you," as she pointed to Anna Mae, "MUST SIGN IN." She moved the visitors sign-in log book, that was on her desk, toward Anna Mae. Anna Mae slid her Gucci shades onto the top of her head, sucking her teeth, grabbing the pen out of the secretary's hand. As she bent over to sign the log book, she said, "I can read! Thank you very much!" Anna Mae tossed the pen down, leaning over the desk until her face was a foot away from the secretary's face and said in a low tone, "Next time, use your indoor voice!" and slid her shades, down, back over her eyes.

Anna Mae turned her nose up and walked over to where David and I were sitting. David, who looked very worried, stood up, leaning against the wall, as Anna Mae stopped directly in front of him. I sat nearby.

"Where's my Momma! What did you two fools do to my Momma?" she barked, this time, removing her shades, holding them delicately in her hand. She scolded us, as if we were the kids that she didn't have, looking at David, then at me and then back at David.

"Don't come at me like that, Anna Mae, with your high sadity self," David growled back at her, raising his voice.

The family sitting across from us huddled together, hugging their two small children as if a fight was about to break out. Anna Mae ignoring David, as she placed her hot pink manicured hand six inches from the tip of his nose "Just STOP!" she said, as she looked my way, "Anyways," She jerked her neck from left to right. She paraded herself in front of the family, who stared at her like she was a demented diva, right before plopping herself right down next to me.

"Oh, my God!" she said, "What do you have on?" looking me up and down. Then it dawned on me. I didn't even think about what I looked like before I ran out of the house in my pink and black floral pajama pants and a gray tank top, that was soiled from the pancake batter. "Please tell me, why are you dressed like a homeless person?" she said, covering her mouth in disbelief, looking embarrassed.

At that moment, I looked down at my chest, remembering that I didn't have on a bra and discreetly folded my arms to hide my perky nipples that were protruding through my tank top.

"Yeah, I'm doing fine Anna Mae? And you?" I said, extremely annoyed by her comments. "Forgive me for cramping your style," I said, rolling my eyes.

David, looking equally annoyed was shaking his head, looking at Anna Mae.

"Enough about you. So, what did the doctor say about Momma?" Anna Mae asked, removing her Gucci eyeglass case from her purse and placing her black Gucci glittered shades into it, putting them safely into her pocketbook.

"All we know is what I told you ten minutes ago when you were in the car coming here. We are waiting for the doctor to come out and give us an update, to that update," I said purposely being smart mouthed. "I tried to call Franklin again after I spoke to you but his commander answered and said that Franklin is in the field this weekend, and won't be back until Monday. He has no way of contacting him," I said.

"Lord have mercy," Anna Mae said, starting with her theatrics. "Poor Franklin is going to have a nervous breakdown when he realizes that you two cannot be trusted to walk Momma to the bathroom."

"Did you call her?" Anna Mae asked.

"Yes, I did. Momma would have wanted her to know," I said.

"So…. did she pick up?" Anna Mae asked, waiting intently to hear my response.

"No," I said. "The message said that her voicemail had not been set up. Besides, don't you think I would have mentioned that to you earlier when we spoke?" I said, getting very annoyed with Anna Mae.

"Yeah, you probably didn't even call her. I see your nose growing," Anna Mae said implying that I was lying.

I knew exactly what to say to Anna Mae, to shut her trap.

"Anna Mae, is Rufus coming in?" I asked sharply.

"No, Grace. He dropped me off and will be back to pick me up," she said and sucked her teeth. "...and stop asking about my husband! Get your own!"

Truth is, I didn't want to see Rufus, as much as he probably didn't want to see me. Whenever Anna Mae wasn't looking, he would say inappropriate comments to me. I told Momma what he was doing, so she always watched him like a hawk when he came around, which was very infrequent.

After Rufus and Anna Mae eloped, Momma had a cookout in the backyard and invited a few people over. I had walked over to the table where Momma had all of the food. As I bent over to reach for a piece of corn on the cob, Rufus came up behind me, out of nowhere, and pressed his bulging privates close against my butt and said, "If you weren't my sister in law," as he reached for a piece of watermelon. He looked me dead in the eyes sucking on it, with the juices running down his ashy hand, peering at me over his cheap dark shades and licking his chapped lips. But when I told Anna Mae, she said I was lying and that I wished that I could have Rufus for myself.

I remember the day when he really crossed the line. I was walking up the stairs in front of him and he had the nerve to pinch my butt and say, "I wish Anna Mae had a fatty like yours." But when I told Anna Mae, she still didn't believe me and said that I probably backed my big round butt, right up into Rufus' hands. Anna Mae just couldn't handle the truth. Her husband was a disgusting pig!

Finally, the double doors, to the room where they wheeled Momma into, opened up. The doctor that had spoken to me and David, appeared and walked toward us.

"Grace Johnson," he said in a loud voice.

"Yes. Over here," Anna Mae said, walking toward the doctor like she was on a runway, her pocketbook swung left to right as if it was trying to keep up with the swaying of her wide hips. David and I finally caught up to her, running behind her like we were her assistants.

"Who are you?" the doctor asked, looking at Anna Mae.

"I'm Anna Mae Johnson. Ms. Leola's oldest daughter. That's who I am," she stated sounding all important.

"Not anymore. You are Anna Mae pain in the a...." David said, as the doctor abruptly cut him off. "It's nice to meet you," the doctor said, shaking Anna Mae's hand.

Ever since Anna Mae got married to Rufus, she only used his last name when it came to applying for credit or making large purchases. Other than that, she refused to have anyone call her, "Mrs. Anna Mae Payne" in public. She took the last name literally and so did we.

"Let's go in here," the doctor said, pointing to the small, dingy looking conference room with gray walls.

We sat down at the coffee stained table.

"Someone needs to come in here and clean this nasty table," Anna Mae said, turning her nose up. "I am about to throw up," she said gagging, holding her hand, daintily over her mouth.

The doctor ignored Anna Mae and gave a half smile as we all sat down at the table.

"As I mentioned earlier, the fall that your mother suffered, resulted in her going into a coma. I've ordered a series of tests to see just how bad of an injury her brain suffered," the doctor explained.

"OH NO!" A theatrical Anna Mae cried out. "Please don't tell me that my Momma is going to be a vegetable for the rest of her life, which means that, I'm going to have to move back into that cramped apartment. Lord knows, these two idiots cannot even take care of themselves," she said looking at me and David.

David stared right back at her. He looked as if he was ready to let loose on Anna Mae. Then quietly, he stood up and walked out, without saying a word.

"Well, let's not put the nail in the coffin yet," the doctor said to Anna Mae.

"From my initial assessment of your mother, it appears that the leukemia has really done a number on her bones and joints and that may have been a huge factor in her fall. However, as I said, until I get the test results back, it is very difficult for me to make an accurate prognosis at this time," the doctor said. David re-entered the room just as the doctor stood up. "Depending on what we find, all of you will need to work together, to decide what's best for your mother," the doctor said looking right at Anna Mae.

"Can I see my Momma?" Anna Mae asked as if she completely ignored the doctor's advice.

The doctor nodded his head and walked out of the room. We all followed behind him.

CHAPTER 8

After Anna Mae and David left the hospital, separately, I sat at Momma's bedside, keeping vigil for hours, waiting for her to wake up. The breathing machine hummed, as I stared at Momma's chest as it rose up and down. There were tubes everywhere. Momma looked so peaceful as if she was sleeping. Her arms rested on each side of her body.

The nurse came in and told me that visiting hours were over but I could stay as long as I wanted. But I decided to head home. I felt so helpless, that the only thing that I could do was say a prayer for Momma before I left her bedside.

By the time I'd made it back to the house, it was 8:45 pm. I took a nice hot shower and put on my favorite button down red dress that Momma bought me last year for my eighteenth birthday, with my red matching lace bra and underwear, that I secretly bought while Momma wasn't looking. It was the last time that Momma and I went shopping together, back when she was able to get around without much assistance. I tied my hair up in my leopard head scarf and I went into the kitchen to fix me something to eat.

I sat at the table in a daze, barely eating the leftover spaghetti and meatballs, that had Momma's signature all over it. I'd helped her the night before, preparing dinner, her hands stiff like a piece of cardboard, as she'd sat in the chair across from me, shaping each meatball into round balls of perfection, sharing stories about her childhood.

It felt so unreal. I was still in shock that Momma was in a coma. I blamed myself for not going in there to help her, instead of sending David. I knew how careless he could be.

David walked into the kitchen, breaking my trance. "I'll be right back," he said.

"Where are you going?" I asked.

"Grace, stop asking me questions like you're Anna Mae. I'm a grown damn man!" he shouted.

"Out! That's where I'm going. I'm going out!" David stormed down the hall, into the living room and slammed the door behind him.

David had been gone for one hour when he'd come back in holding a brown paper bag.

"David, what is that? Is that liquor?" I asked.

"Mind your business, Grace. You are not the only one who is stressed around here," he said. I watched him remove the unopened bottle of Hennessy out of the bag, open it and take a sip.

"David, you know that Momma said no liquor in the house," I reminded him.

"Grace. Shut the hell up!" He snapped back at me. "Your momma is in the hospital in a coma. She cannot stop me and neither can you!" He yelled.

David had a way of being so mean, especially when it came to me defending Momma and her house rules.

David walked over to the stereo. He took out Momma's CD of Mahalia Jackson, replacing it with his CD and turned the volume up, putting it on blast. The loud rap music that Momma banned him from listening to, echoed throughout the house. I could feel the vibration of the large speakers, coming up through the floor.

I didn't know who David had turned into.

Or maybe the thought of Momma not coming out of her coma, and him having to get a job to take care of himself, was really sinking in.

I couldn't stand to watch him disappoint Momma any longer so I walked onto the porch to get some fresh air.

I could hear Big Tuna below me, on the first floor chatting it up with a woman but I couldn't make out what she was saying. Nor, did I recognize her voice. Big Tuna was Old Man Joe's 24-year-old son, who stayed with him when he wasn't locked up in prison.

Big Tuna had done some time, for allegedly beating up his girlfriend and stealing checks out of people's mailboxes. He was a good 235lbs and stood 6'2" inches tall. He looked like a walking billboard, with tattoos covering every inch of his body that was visible, including the dagger with the cyclops on the side of his face.

I leaned over the railing, out of sight, listening to their conversation. I heard Big Tuna say something about getting some tonight, to celebrate his five years out the pen. I didn't know what he was referring to, but both, he and the woman laughed.

I walked back into the house to David trying to sing Rappers Delight, looking like a wannabe member of the Sugar Hill Gang. "And the next on the mic is my man Hank c'mon, Hank, sing that song, check it out." I walked by him and he placed the bottle of Hennessy directly in front of my lips using the bottle as a microphone like Franklin and I use to do with my hairbrush. "Sing Hank," he said to me, laughing hysterically.

I pushed the bottled out of my face, shook my head and walked to my bedroom, disgusted by David's blatant disrespect to Momma's house rules and to me. I shut my bedroom door behind me and laid on my bed staring at the ceiling. Just the thought of Momma not coming back and me having to deal with this disrespectful knucklehead, opened up the flood gate of tears.

I put the blanket over my head and cried myself to sleep.

CHAPTER 9

I shot straight up, out of my sleep after having a bad dream about Momma's fate. I felt as if, I'd been asleep for hours. I looked over at the clock sitting on my crème dresser that read 11:35 pm. Oddly, the house was very quiet and I didn't hear David or his music. Maybe he drank himself into a stupor and was laying on the kitchen floor dead somewhere. That was wishful thinking, on my part. I opened my bedroom door to see the entire house pitch black.

"David? David?" I called out.

I knocked on David's bedroom door, that was ajar before opening it up. The glow from his fluorescent blue clock, illuminated his room, giving me enough light, to see inside his room. As I walked toward his dresser, I tripped over the empty bottle of Hennessy, that he had bought earlier and I fell onto his bed.

I regained my balance and walked out of David's room. As I walked down the hall, I noticed a streak of light creeping in through the front door, into the living room, that I hadn't noticed before going into David's room. The light switch was on the other side of the room, so it remained dark.

Why would this dummy leave the apartment and not close the door behind him, I wondered? Unless he misplaced his house key, I thought, shaking my head.

"David. David. Are you here?" I called out again.

I heard the creaky door from the storage closet in the hall slowly open.

Those daggone cats! Old Man Joe couldn't pay his rent on time but he had no problem spending his money on cat food, feeding all of the stray cats in the neighborhood. A few strays must have taken up residence in our storage closet, I figured. I had shooed two out of the hallway, just yesterday. All of a sudden I heard what sounded like a foot step.

In a split-second, fear came over me.

I walked slowly toward the door to shut it, trying not to make a noise. But just as I put my hand on the doorknob, a boot was wedged in the door.

I stood there, frozen.

His large frame blocked the light, making it impossible for me to see his face. I tried to push him out but his strength was no match for my small frame.

"NOOO!" I screamed. "Get out!" I screamed again. This time hoping that someone nearby would hear me.

He didn't say a word as he forced his way inside of the door, overpowering me with all of his might.

He threw me on the floor and ripped my favorite red dress clean off of my body; my silver buttons popped off like popcorn.

I repeatedly beat on his chest.

With one hand, he grabbed ahold of my laced red bra and pulled it so hard that my bra straps snapped and my perfect breasts sprung straight up in the air.

"No!" I screamed. "Please!" I begged. I tried helplessly to fight him off.

"Get off of me!" I said.

We rolled back and forth. I tried to knee him in the nuts, just as the instructor had taught me from the self-defense class when I was in school.

Nothing worked. He put his warm, nasty mouth on my breasts, licking them and then he bit down hard, on my nipple.

I screamed so loud. The pain was excruciating.

His body weighed me down, just as my mind had been all day.

I thought of Momma. I needed her right now.

I cried. I screamed. I kicked. I fought with everything inside of me.

Then he did the unthinkable. He reached toward my private area. Fondling me. He stuck his finger inside of me, then took it out and shoved his moist finger right in my mouth.

I gagged.

He removed his finger out of my mouth and forcefully tried to kiss me.

I turned my face from left to right. "NO!" I screamed again, but I was weak. I had no more fight in me.

"Stop! Leave me alone!"

My life flashed before me.

I wondered, where was my brother. I needed him right now more than I ever needed him before.

I screamed his name, "David! David! HELP!"

All of a sudden, this monster, pulled my red laced panties to the side.

I felt him, all of him, inside of me.

I screamed, to the top of my lungs, "NOOOOOOOOO! Stop! You're hurting me."

Finally, he'd had enough of me.

He punched me so hard, on the right side of my face, that I blacked out.

CHAPTER 10

My body fell limp in the hallway on the first floor. He then dragged me outside, onto the front porch, down the four steps and dropped me on the ground, after seeing the car pull up. He disappeared, running off into the darkness. I tried to stumble after him but collapsed in the middle of the road.

I faintly heard a woman's voice yelling in the distance, "Who's over there? You better get from behind them bushes before I pistol whip you!"

"Help, help me," I said faintly as I coughed up a little blood.

"OH, MY GOD," the woman said rushing over to me.

"Wake up. Wake up!" the woman exclaimed slapping my face.

I opened my eyes to the brightness of her car headlights. My entire body, felt as if I had gotten hit by a Mack truck.

"You need to go to the doctors," she said trying to help me up.

"No! Where am I?" I asked her. She held my head like Momma would.

"You were in the middle of the road but I scared off whoever had attacked you. I almost ran right over you, as I parked," the woman said. As I began to stand up she helped me, wrapping my ripped dress, with no buttons, around me, attempting to keep it closed.

"Thank you," I said. As I tried to find my bearings. I was thankful it was finally over.

"Oh, my God, honey you have blood running down your leg," she said.

"And your eye is swelling. I'm calling the police!" she exclaimed.

"No!" I said. "I live in that apartment building right there, on the second floor." I pointed my sore hand toward Momma's apartment, which happened to be directly across the street, not far from where she found me.

"Please, just take me home. My brother can take me to the hospital" I begged.

Reluctantly, the woman walked me to Momma's apartment. Holding onto her for dear life, I limped all the way there. As we reached the top of the steps, I could barely make out from the hallway, the apartment door, which appeared to be open about a foot. She slowly pushed it wide open. "Where's the light?" she asked. She glided her hand up and down the wall, searching for the light switch.

"It's right there," I said pointing to the direction of the light switch, as I sat down slowly on the recliner across from the couch.

Eventually, she found the switch and flipped on the dim light, that seemed to shine so bright.

"Oh boy. You look like you got hit by a 2x4. Are you sure you don't want me to call the police?" she asked again.

My eyes were a blur. I could hear her but I couldn't make out who this good Samaritan was.

"No," I said shyly. "My brother should be home soon. I will have him take me to the hospital." Truth was, I couldn't bear sitting at the hospital another minute after spending most of the day there with Momma.

"Who do you live here with besides your brother?" she asked.

My head started pounding from all that I had been through. "My Momma," I answered softly.

"Where is she? Do you want me to call her?" she asked, looking around the apartment.

"My mother is in the hospital and I don't know where my brother David is. He should be back soon," I said with hope.

"Well, you should really go get yourself checked out," she said.

"I will," I responded.

"Do you mind if I check to see if David is here," she said.

"No," I said holding onto my head.

"David!" she yelled. Her voice sent my head into a tail spin as if someone had swung me around a hundred times.

The woman began to walk down the hall as if she had been here before. She headed right to David's room, "David. Are you in here?" she said. I tried to focus my eyes but my vision was very blurry. I couldn't make out her face and her voice didn't sound familiar to me but her perfume smelled really nice, like Sunkist oranges.

She came back out to the front of the apartment, walking toward me. "Your brother is not here. I even checked the closet. So, I'll see myself out."

Holding my head down in my hands, the only thing I could see was her bright orange croc shoes, as they clicked right on passed me, straight toward the door.

She stopped, turned around and said, "Take care of those bruises," and closed the door behind her.

CHAPTER II

The next morning, I rolled out of bed, trying to remember what had happened last night. I felt like Old Man Joe. I couldn't remember anything! I vaguely remembered waiting for David to come in. My body felt as if it had been rolled over ten times by a steamroller. I slowly rolled off of the bed and made my way into the bathroom. I could barely see out of my right eye. As I passed by the mirror, I got a glimpse of my battered and bruised face.

"Oh, my God! What happened to me?" I couldn't believe what I looked like. It looked as if I went a couple of rounds with Laila Ali and she definitely won.

I felt the puffy area around my bruised and swollen eye. It was tender to the touch and black and blue in color.

I could not let anyone see me like this. I reached into the drawer and pulled out the MAC makeup that Anna Mae forgot that she hid in the bathroom drawer and tried to hide my scars.

I remember when a baseball socked Franklin in the eye, Momma placed a cold rag onto his eye.

I headed to Momma's bedroom, for some tender, love and care. I suddenly stopped in my tracks, forgetting that she was not there. I looked at her empty bed, as sadness came over me. I leaned against Momma's bedroom door and sobbed; wishing I could turn back the hands of time before Momma's fall. I wanted nothing more but to have my Momma home back where she belonged. I held my sore face down, into the palm of my hands.

The house phone rang off the hook until I walked slowly into the kitchen to answer it. My entire body feeling numb.

"Hello," I said, trying to disguise my voice, to not let on that I'd been bawling my eyes out.

"Are you just waking up? It's almost noon," Anna Mae asked not giving me a chance to respond.

"Where were you last night? I called you several times and you didn't pick up," she said.

As I tried to get my bearings, I responded, "I was here? Why?" Sounding unsure of my whereabouts.

She paused or maybe she was multitasking and busy. But there was a brief silence of which I filled with an, "Oh I fell asleep," as if my memory was coming back.

"Well, I spoke to David. I don't know what time it was and he didn't say that," she said.

"Well of course not, because we had an argument, after he brought alcohol in Momma's house, knowing that she asked him not to," I said.

Anna Mae gave no response or sympathy to my complaint.

"Well, anyways, after you left the hospital, the nurse called me and said she tried to get in contact with you to see if you could come back and pick up Momma's diamond earrings before she got off her shift so they wouldn't get stolen." Anna Mae said. "I don't know why you didn't take them diamond earrings out of Momma's ear."

"Well Anna Mae, it's probably because, after her fall, I was more concerned with getting her help, than what she had on!" I shouted. I was getting angry with Anna Mae. "Besides, didn't you see them when you were wailing all over Momma's head at the hospital yesterday?"

"Well, anyways!" Anna Mae said, ignoring my questions. "I finally got David on his cell phone and he said that you were at the house. I assumed he was too," she said.

"He went out." I snapped back, not mentioning that he stupidly left the door open.

"Whatever! The both of you are going buck wild, now that Momma is not there to watch you both like a hawk," she assumed.

"Is that it? I gotta go!" I said. I had enough of her and started to feel like I needed to sit down.

"Rufus said he came by there to drop off Momma's earrings but the apartment was pitch dark, but he saw Momma's car parked out in front. So, he came back home and gave me Momma's earrings," she said.

I didn't dare mention to Anna Mae, that David's license was suspended. It wasn't my business to tell. As long as he didn't take Momma's car, I was good. Wherever he went, he was on foot.

"Okay. I got to go Anna Mae," I didn't even wait for her to say goodbye, I just hung up the phone.

I couldn't take her judgment any longer so I walked down the hall into the living room. The air was filled with the all too familiar sound of David's loud snoring and the unfamiliar smell of alcohol. David was sprawled out on the couch; thick drool hanging out of his mouth. His snoring sounding more like a revved-up car engine. He laid there, looking more like he was dead than asleep, wreaking of alcohol. Another bottle of Hennessy was beside him on the floor, empty. This bottle was bigger than the one that I tripped over in his room last night. I wanted so bad to pick up the empty bottle and crack it over David's head for not telling me that he was going out and for leaving the door open, resulting in the brutal assault on me. But I couldn't even do it if I wanted to. Every muscle in my body hurt. My entire body was throbbing. I wasn't quite sure what had happened to me but I knew that it was time for me to go to the hospital.

In between David's snores, I heard voices from outside. I slowly walked over and pulled back the curtain to find our dead-end street lit up like a Christmas tree. The cops had blocked it off, not allowing anyone but an ambulance truck to enter. Five police cruisers were in front of the house, of the woman who I think found me. I watched two police officers, as they stretched the, "Do Not Cross," tape in front of the entrance of her home, while one of the other officers guided the EMT's into the house.

I could see the Channel 5 camera crew parked near the entrance of our street. A news reporter stood toward the corner of the house interviewing Old Man Joe, as he pointed his cane, up in the direction of our two-family apartment building. Fifteen minutes later, I saw them roll a body out on a stretcher. Although a sheet covered the dead body, I could see the bottom of the deceased; bright orange bloodied croc shoes.

"Oh, my God!" I gasped.

CHAPTER 12

Four months had passed since Momma fell into a coma. It was also four months since my vicious sexual assault and the mysterious death of the woman who came to my rescue. Her house had become an attraction to the neighborhood kids, who'd stand in front of it, taking selfies, as if it was part of an eerie Stephen King movie. I couldn't help but think that whoever assaulted me and left me for dead in the middle of the street, killed the woman who helped me, thinking that she would be able to recognize him. What had happened to me and the woman, had paralyzed me so, that I only left the house, if it was absolutely necessary.

For a few months after the incident, the cops had come knocking on a few of the neighbor's doors trying to get any information that they could, that might have led up to her death. I wanted so much to tell them what I knew but I was deathly afraid to tell anyone what happened to me, nor did I want to mention my encounter with the woman in fear of the perpetrator coming to kill me next. Besides, when Momma wasn't home, we were used to pretending as if we were not home either. Especially if it was someone that we were not expecting, like the Jehovah Witnesses.

I felt all alone. Not able to tell Franklin, Anna Mae or David what I had gone through. Somehow, as strange as it may sound, Anna Mae would have sworn up and down, that I did something or said something to cause the assault.

The relationship amongst us siblings had become strained in more ways than one. We were pointing the finger at each other, blaming one another for each other's shortcomings, drudging up the past that none of us could change, instead of coming together to do what was in the best interest of Momma. Each one of us talking over one another to try to prove our point. Not to mention that the secret that I was holding, weighed me down like a ton of bricks.

After seeing my older siblings show no mercy with throwing me or each other under the bus, I knew that this was nothing that I was ready to share with them no time soon. Anna Mae had a way of hypnotizing Franklin into siding with her but I knew, in a matter of time, he would eventually snap out of it. The two of them, pretty much stuck together, blaming me and David for Momma's accident and only called around the first of the month, just to make sure that we went down to collect the rent from Old Man Joe. That was pretty much the only time that I spoke to David, just to remind him. I'd stopped going downstairs to get the rent from Old Man Joe. After Momma's accident, on two occasions he came to the door in only his boxers, making me feel very uncomfortable. Especially the time that he grabbed his crotch, like he was Michael Jackson, asking me if I wanted to come in and keep him company. I don't know what David said or did to put Old Man Joe in check but whatever it was, it worked. He didn't bother me after that. I think he was just lonely.

Although Anna Mae left us in the dark, she'd pretty much taken over all of Momma's affairs, only sharing things with me and David, on a, "need to know," basis. I prayed that she was paying Momma's bills on time. I dreaded the day that David and I would come find a padlock on the front door. I spent most of my evenings holding a vigil, sitting by Momma's bedside, when I wasn't too scared to leave the house. The only thing that had changed in Momma's condition, was that she had lost a lot of weight. She was a fraction of the woman that she used to be.

Anna Mae had annoyed the doctor, so much, that they had blocked her phone number. For the past four months that Momma lay in the hospital, Anna Mae had been calling the hospital every other day, disguising her voice, demanding an update on Momma's health; instead of getting off her butt and going to the hospital to see her.

Since Momma hadn't made any real progress from the coma and had been kept alive by a feeding tube and breathing machine, the doctor had requested that he meet with us to decide what was best for Momma. Because of Momma's Christian beliefs, she'd always told us, that if something were to ever happen to her, that she didn't want to be on no feeding tube and didn't want no machine keeping her alive but this was Anna Mae's idea and not even Franklin, as the oldest, was able to sway her decision.

I dreaded the day that we had to sit down and talk to the doctor. The thought of losing Momma and not ever seeing her again pained me in such huge way. When we got to the hospital, me, Franklin, Anna Mae, and David met before we spoke to the doctor and made the decision, considering Momma's wishes.

Since Anna Mae was so bossy, me, Franklin and David allowed her to be the spokesperson for all of us. Sadness filled the air like thick smog, as Anna Mae told the doctor that we agreed to take Momma off of life support and that Momma had suffered long enough.

As Anna Mae was talking, my stomach started to feel queasy. I hadn't said anything, but for the past few months, ever since that awful day, that I've been unable to erase out of my mind, I'd been throwing up. Even at nineteen, I knew what sex was even though Momma made it a point to not tell me and Anna Mae nothing, outside of, "keep your legs closed and your dress tail down." My face had been filling out. The clothes that I had been wearing for the past year, had become snug. I no longer looked like Toni Braxton's twin but more like Anita Baker. My once finicky appetite had disappeared and I was eating everything in sight. As I drowned Anna Mae out, with my racing thoughts, I sat in the chair, as I grieved for not only Momma but for the old me. One thing was for sure, I had to stop at the store later and pick up a pregnancy test.

CHAPTER 13

The doctor led us into Momma's hospital room.

"I'll give you all some time to say your good-byes," he said walking out of the room and into the hall.

Anna Mae began to wail as if she started to feel guilty. "Momma. I'm sorry! I'm going to miss you, Momma."

I gave her the side eye. The last time Momma called Anna Mae to come help her, Anna Mae, who don't drive nothing but everyone crazy, said to Momma "You'll have to ask my husband since he has to drive me."

I looked across at Franklin. As usual he was strong and silent. He stood statuesque in his Army fatigues, as he held onto Momma's hand looking more like a defeated fighter, who had just gotten knocked out in the first round. As usual, David was sitting on his butt, slouched in a chair looking more hungover than anything. He held his head down as he slowly removed his Ray-burn aviator sunglasses from his shirt pocket, putting them on to hide his red eyes. I didn't know if he was mourning Momma or the fact that he would have to get a job and take care of himself for now on.

I stood at the foot of Momma's bed. My mind starting racing. Even though Momma had been in the hospital for the past four months, I never imagined my life without her in it. Tears started to roll down my eye and stream down my full cheeks. I not only hurt for what Momma had been through, but I hurt for what I had been through too. In this moment, life seemed so unfair; I had so many regrets. I was angry at the monster who did this to me. I regretted not going to the hospital. And now, I could possibly be pregnant with no other choice but to keep my baby or give it up for adoption. With all of these thoughts running through my mind, Momma's doctor re-entered the room, with the nurse following behind him.

"It's time," he said.

Every part of my body stiffened. My heart sank to the floor.

We watched as the nurse unhooked the tubes from Momma's body. Momma looked so peaceful as if she was sleeping.

"I will always love you, Momma," I whispered.

Momma took her last breath.

Then, she was gone.

Chapter 14

_____

I walked up to the booth, that read "Consultation," directly under the rather large Pharmacy sign.

"How can I help you," the pharmacy assistant asked from the other side of the booth, popping her chewing gum that smelled like cinnamon. The smell made my stomach queasy, which gave me the hint that I was pregnant since Big Red was my favorite brand of gum.

"I'm looking for the pregnancy tests," I whispered.

"Honey. You are going to have to speak up a bit louder. I'm hard of hearing in my left year," the seemingly ghetto pharmacy assistant said, "and I am not good at reading lips; since these old eyes are failing me," The woman looked to be about Momma's age, reaching for her bifocals. "I think I'm pregnant," I said. "What aisle can I find the pregnancy tests in?" I asked.

"Well, congratulations," the woman said, popping her chewing gum after each word. She jumped up and came from around the booth, waddling, slapping me on the back. "I can't walk that fast now. My sciatica is acting up, got my legs in so much pain, I'm gonna need a cane directly," she said.

I thought to myself, if she only knew that I had a mountain of my own issues. I had just lost my Momma and think I may be pregnant by someone who had sexually assaulted me, that I didn't even know. Not to mention, that the image of that beast haunted me daily and it definitely didn't feel like, Casper the friendly ghost was visiting, and I definitely was not in any congratulatory spirit! I followed the woman to the aisle where the pregnancy tests were.

"This one here is a good one," she recommended. She picked up the Clearblue pregnancy test. "See this here," she said pointing to the picture on the front, looking over her glasses. "It says, pregnant, not pregnant, you know, that's how you'll know. All you got to do is pee on the stick and…"

Not allowing her to finish.

"I know what to do," I said.

Truth is, I didn't but I did know how to read.

"I'll get that one," I said, grabbing one of the boxes out of her hand trying to hurry up and get out of the aisle before someone recognized me.

"Ok, baby. You know we do consultations if you have any more questions," the pharmacist said, with her hands on her hips.

"Ok, thanks," I said as I hurried away from her.

Just as I turned the corner, I bumped right into Misty.

"Oh, my God, Grace! How are you? I haven't seen you in a long time. Look at that bush," she said referring to my head full of natural hair.

"Oh, hi Misty," I said trying to hide the box behind my leg.

"Girl you have got to come into the salon, so I can do this hair of yours," Misty said, attempting to fix the fly away strands that danced all over my head. I stood there feeling as if, I'd gone from having one consultation to another. Misty had finished high school when she was only seventeen, graduating at the top of her class. She went off to beauty school and now at 21, she owned her own hair salon and was known as one of the best hair stylists in the city.

Misty met Momma when she was fifteen. Momma would see her waiting for the BAT bus, early in the mornings, on her way to her doctor appointments, before she became too sick to drive herself. When the weather was bad, Momma would often stop to give Misty a ride to the bus station, so she wouldn't be late for school. Misty's mother refusing to put her in public school, put her in an all-girls school way out in Wellesley. So, when Misty opened up her own hair salon, nearby to where we lived, Momma became one of her biggest cheerleaders and loyal customers, admiring her strong work ethic. When Momma was too sick to get to the salon, Misty would come by, after she closed the shop and do Momma's hair for free, but Momma would try to give Misty something in return, like a spiced, carrot cake or some Red Velvet cupcakes, Misty's favorite.

One day, when Misty was over doing Momma's hair, Misty shared with us, that her mother had told her, back when she was fourteen, that she was adopted and how she dreamed of one day, trying to locate her birth parents and seeing if she had any siblings. She wanted to see if she resembled any of them. Her adopted mother didn't tell her much but since the records were no longer sealed, once she turned twenty-one, she said that, once she found some time, she was going to make it her business to locate her birth relatives. She said that she was not angry that her adopted mother never told her before since she had a good life and wanted for nothing. That day, Momma vowed to help her, in any way that she could.

As I stood in the store, a feeling of sorrow came over me, because I knew that Momma would never get that chance to help Misty fulfill her dream of finding her family.

"I saw your Mother's car outside. How's Ms. Leola doing? You know she's like a second mother to me," Misty said smiling. "I miss her. The last time she stopped by the shop to say hi, she wasn't getting around too well," she said, her expression going from happy to a deeply concerned look. "Is she in here with you Grace?" Misty said, looking around the area, with hopes of spotting Momma. Since Misty was like family to us, I didn't mind sharing Momma's business with her.

"Well, Momma had a bad fall four months ago and she fell into a coma. We just got back from the hospital," I told her trying not to cry.

"Oh, my gosh Grace. I'm so sorry! Is she okay?" Misty said, placing her hand over her heart. "What's the doctor's saying? I need to go see Ms. Leola. Which hospital is she in?" Misty asked appearing deeply disturbed and not allowing me to answer any of her questions.

"Momma died. We took her off of life support today." I said somberly.

"What? She's DEAD?" Misty said, sounding shocked, covering her mouth with both hands. "What happened? Why didn't any of you call and tell me?" she asked.

"I'm so sorry Misty," I said. "We didn't say anything, hoping that Momma would come out of the coma," I said. "I guess we were all in denial. Momma's condition wasn't improving and we just couldn't stand to see her suffer like that. So, me, Franklin, Anna Mae and David decided to take her off of life support today."

I knew that nothing that I said, could snap Misty out of the shock that she was in. I was surprised that Misty didn't hear about Momma's accident. In the small city that we live in, Momma was well known for her baked goods and running the soup kitchen down at the church. News about her accident would have been the topic of any salon or barber shop conversation because she was so well liked. Momma had a good heart and would often bake a batch of her delicious chocolate chip or oatmeal raisin cookies and drop them by all of the black owned businesses, she knew of. It was her way of letting them know that she supported them. Up until her accident, she did her best to keep up her ritual, even when she was not feeling one hundred percent, having David drop them off for her.

"I am so sorry, Grace!" Misty said with tears in her eyes. She pulled me in so close for a hug that her pocketbook hit the pregnancy test, sending the box falling right out of my hand and onto the floor.

Misty's eyes were full of tears.

I scrambled down to pick up the box before she could notice it but Misty's keen eyes caught the big blue writing on the box.

"Grace, are you pregnant!" she exclaimed "OH MY GOD!" she said, pulling me in for another hug, this one not as forceful as the first and felt more like a, "I feel sorry for you," type of hug.

"I may be," I said, sounding unsure.

The puzzled look that Misty had on her face, looked as if she was putting the pieces together.

"Oh, my God Grace! Ms. Leola didn't' know!" She said.

"No," I said, my eyes shifting to the floor, as I starting to relive that awful day.

"Did you tell Anna Mae?" She asked.

Misty knew that was a dumb question. Anna Mae bad mouthed me so bad at the salon, making up lies about me, to make herself look innocent, that she had me looking like I was a fast tail, promiscuous hussy, with no morals or standards, giving my cookies out for free, for a dribble of someone's milk.

"No! None of my siblings know. I don't even know for sure," I said shrugging my shoulders. I've been throwing up for the past three months and I haven't gotten my period" I said.

"Oh, Grace. I'm so sorry," she said, reaching for my empty hand, holding it tight.

That's what I loved about Misty, she was not judgmental. She was not concerned with who got me pregnant, not that I even knew. She was so different from Anna Mae in every way. She treated me as if she cared.

She was like the sister that I wish I had.

"Grace. Why don't you pay for that," she said pointing at the box, "and I'll meet you up front. Then we can go into the bathroom and check it together," she said, picking up on the terrifying look that I had. "Your mother would not want you to go through this by yourself and you know that you can trust me," She said, hugging me around my shoulders.

A bit of my sadness subsided. I didn't feel so alone anymore. I felt that there was a reason why I bumped into Misty, of all people. It was as if Momma had become my angel and sent her my way. After paying for the pregnancy test, I stood near the bathroom and waited for Misty, who was in the checkout line. Even though she was only two years older than me, she carried herself as if she was in her 30's. She was wise beyond her years and had a certain sureness about herself that I envied, in a good way.

"Hey Mr. Carter," Misty said, as she put her Cheetos and slim fast up on the counter.

Misty was beautiful. She had a coke bottle shape, similar to the body that I had four months ago before I got knocked up. Her body was toned, just like Jada Pinkett Smith's. The last time that I saw her, she was wearing a long blonde weave but she'd replaced it with her own natural, shoulder length thick hair, that she wore in dreads, with the ends dyed platinum blonde. Her maroon, off the shoulder maxi dress, fitted her body like a glove and accented all of her curves. Her chunky gold chain link necklace and matching bracelet added the perfect finishing touch.

"Thank you, Mr. Carter. Can you put my bag behind the counter? I'll be right back," she said, as she sashayed toward me.

Mr. Carter followed her firm-round booty, with his eyes, as if her butt was a basketball.

"Can I get some fries with that shake?" he said, licking his lips, as she walked away. She looked back and smiled, paying him no mind. Everything she did exuded confidence.

We disappeared behind the big red door, leading to the ladies' room. Misty and I stood at the sink, staring at the stick, as if it were a crystal ball, as we waited for it to tell me my future.

"What did the box say again?" I said looking at the instructions.

Misty looked at me, as if she was teaching me a history lesson, "Girl, it's simple, you pee on the stick and it will tell you if you are pregnant or not," she said, sounding as if she had experience.

"Okay. I got it," I said.

"Grace, if you are pregnant, you will need to make an appointment to get you and the baby checked out," she said.

"Okay. I'll call Dr. Shaw's office and set up an appointment if I am," I said.

Misty laughed, "Grace, isn't Dr. Shaw the pediatrician, with the big billboard downtown?" she asked.

"Yes," I said.

"Honey, you will need to go to an obstetrician," she said.

"A who?" I said.

Misty laughed, "An obstetrician specializes in caring for women who are pregnant," she said, as she hugged me. "I wouldn't expect you to know that, since you've never been pregnant before."

I looked at her as if I was the student and she was the teacher.

"Oh, my God!" She exclaimed, looking at the stick.

"Grace, you're pregnant!"

CHAPTER 15

I sat in the car, as I banged my head on the steering wheel, disappointed in myself, for not going to the hospital months ago. I wished that I hadn't been so scared that what happened to the woman, was going to happen to me. Blaming David, if he hadn't left the door open for the perpetrator to come in, I would not be in this situation. My sadness turned into anger. I needed to find out who did this to me. He had to pay. Why would he hurt me in such a brutal way and then leave me half naked in the street?

I tried hard to remember what happened that night but it was still such a blur.

Not only did I lose my Momma, but this evil person robbed me of my future.

I hit my head against the steering wheel. I wanted to die.

Within an instant, something came over me. It was as if something was stirring up in me. It suddenly made me feel empowered. I knew that I had to speak up so that this doesn't happen to anyone else. I closed my eyes and rested my head on the head rest.

"Knock, knock," I opened my eyes and jumped from the bang on the car window. The sound startled me. It was Old Man Joe banging his cane on my window.

Old Man Joe was standing outside of the car door, holding a fire engine red shopping bag, wearing a gray Fedora, with an oversized, navy blue wool sports jacket, pin-striped red and white pants and some Converse classic chuck, white high top sneakers, looking like a hot mess. It was way too many layers, for this unusual sixty degree, November day.

I rolled down the window.

"Hi, Old Man Joe," I said.

"Yeah, I'm here to pick up my blood pressure pills," he said.

Old Man Joe had got my window mixed up with the walk-up pharmacy window, that was ten feet in front of where I'd parked.

"Old Man Joe, the window is over there," I said pointing to the big sign that said, "Walk Up, Pick Up Here."

"How you know my name, gal?" he asked, darting away from me and walking toward the pick-up window. Not recognizing that it was me.

I must admit, I kind of felt bad for the old man, knowing that at one point in his life, his mind was probably as sharp as any tack that held up a Post-it note and now, his memory was more like a bowl of mush.

I watched Old Man Joe, as he stuffed his prescription into his bright red shopping bag and walked back towards my way.

"Old Man Joe," I yelled. "Come on, I'll drop you off at home."

"Gal, I don't know you," he said walking toward me, as I sat in the car.

As he got closer he said, "Grace girl, is that you? You sure did turn out pretty. I'm glad you finally got rid of them coke bottle glasses. Them things made you look like Grace Jones," Old Man Joe cracked up laughing, obviously getting me mixed up with Anna Mae.

"Bring me to the chicken house," he said, opening the passenger's side door and getting into the backseat.

I felt just like Momma and didn't have the energy to fuss with Old Man Joe, who apparently, in an instant, thought I was an Uber driver.

"Do you mean Flo's Finger Lickin' Fried Chicken?" I asked.

"Yeah! that'll do. Maybe you can drop me off at that Hot Slots Casino too! I feel lucky today gal," he said, scratching his left palm. "How much is the fair?"

"For you, it's free, today," I said shaking my head.

I drove out of the parking lot, contemplating if I should tell Old Man Joe about Momma. I looked in the rearview mirror and he was fast asleep.

Old Man Joe woke up when I drove over the speed bump.

"Gal, you trying to kill me?" he said holding onto the arm of the door.

He looked at the large brown and yellow sign, that read Flo's Finger Lickin' Fried Chicken, "Gal, this ain't Fifi's Fried Chicken," he said.

"You said you wanted to go to Flo's Finger Lickin' Fried Chicken," I said, "There are no Fifi's Fried Chicken in this city."

"Gal, if this chicken sends me to the toilet, I'm gonna come looking for you, ya' hear," he said, shaking the handle of his cane at me. Old Man Joe opened the door and got out of the car.

Before he shut the door, he leaned down into the car saying, "Now don't you go getting out. I ain't got no money to feed the both of us and I don't want the smell of the chicken to make you hungry," then he shut the car door.

Old Man Joe was a welcomed distraction from what I had just gone through in the past 24 hours but he couldn't erase the uncalming storm that was brewing inside of me.

I sat in the car, waiting for Old Man Joe, thinking of how I should tell Franklin, Anna Mae & David what happened to me and that I was pregnant.

My cell phone rang.

"Hello," I said.

"Grace, where are you?" Speaking of the devil, it was Anna Mae.

"You need to get Mommas car back here. Now that she's gone, you are not to be going buck wild, gallivanting all up in the street," she said.

"Anna Mae, no one is gallivanting all up in the street. I'm running old Man Joe on an errand," I said.

"What? You need to get that old, nasty, smelly man out of Momma's car right now! He smells like he don't bathe," she snarled.

"Anna Mae, what is it to you! You don't even have your license! The only thing you know how to do is drive people CRAZY!" I yelled at her.

Click.

Anna Mae hung up on me.

I tossed my phone in my pocket book and looked up just in time, to see that Old Man Joe had already come out of Flo's Finger Lickin' Fried Chicken restaurant and walked right past me, not even realizing he'd walked by the car. I watched him, following behind a girl, who'd also come out of the restaurant.

She must have sensed him. She turned around and yelled, "Get away from me, you dirty old man!"

Old Man Joe, tried to balance his box of chicken, as he lifted his cane, aiming straight for her jiggly butt.

"I'll tap that…"

"Old Man Joe!" I yelled before he could finish. "I'm over here." He looked over in my direction and said, "Gal, you gonna get enough of playing musical cars on me!"

CHAPTER 16

I pulled up in front of our apartment. I looked over at Old Man Joe, who had fallen asleep in that short ride back to the house. This time, he had stretched out, across the entire backseat. The crumbs from the chicken, that he ate while I was driving, was stuck to his lapel as if he forgot where his mouth was.

"Old Man Joe, wake up. We are back at the house," I said.

Old Man Joe woke up giggling like a horny teenager, as he sat up in the backseat.

"Girl did you see Cookie undressing me with her eyes. I told her to come and get it," he said licking his lips, as he tried to discretely take his dentures out of the inside of his jacket pocket, popping them back into his mouth.

I know that my facial expression said it all but my mind said, YUCK!

Old Man Joe, looked around, "Oh, this looks familiar," he said, as if he just came out of a time warp.

"Hold on now," he said, as he reached into his bright red shopping bag pulling out his wallet. "Gal you know I'm not rich. Your Momma done took every red cent I had saved up in my penny jar, but I want to give you something for your troubles, you know, to let ya know that I appreciate ya."

"Old Man Joe, you do not have to pay me. We were going the same way," I said.

"Now don't you do it. You woman just need to shut up and learn how to take it," he said. For a minute, I didn't know if Old Man Joe even knew what he was saying.

"Now here gal. Take this here and you go head and get that hair done of yours. You riding me around looking like a little dark-skinned troll," he said as he handed me $10 in food stamps, over the front seat.

"I'm good," I said, refusing to take the food stamps.

Right about now, I had enough of Old Man Joe. Even a roll of toilet paper has its limit.

I opened the car door and started to get out when I noticed Big Tuna walk out onto the porch, with a straw hanging out of his mouth, looking pissed. He must've gotten locked out of the house again. Old Man Joe refused to give him a key but there had been a few times when he would wedge the heavy metal door open with a brick.

"Come on Old Man. Hurry up and get out the car. I gotta piss," he said. He spoke very rudely to Old Man Joe, continuing to jump up and down like a little kid, about to pee on himself.

"Yo, Grace. Real talk, thanks for looking out for my pops," he said.

I looked at him surprised. I didn't know that Big Tuna knew my name. He usually addressed me as, "Shorty,"

"No problem," I said. Making it over to the passenger side. I carefully reached under Old Man Joe's arm, helping him onto the sidewalk.

"Gal, don't you try to goose me," he said, laughing, clucking his arm like a chicken.

"What does that mean?" I asked.

"Don't pay my Daddy no mind," Big Tuna said. He made that face just like Ice Cube, when he lifts his top lip up, almost touching his nose.

"She ain't trying to tickle your old behind," Big Tuna said.

"Just give me the key," he said. Then Big Tuna snatched the key right out of Old Man Joe's hand.

The key dropped out of Old Man Joe's fragile hands. I reached down to get it, noticing that Big Tuna was wearing timberlands.

I froze.

The person who assaulted me wore the same foot wear; I'll never forget it!

"Shorty, you gotta go too?" Big Tuna asked, aware that I had suddenly stopped right in my tracks.

"No, I don't," I said, in a low voice.

"You can use our bathroom if you can't make it upstairs. That's the least I could do," he said and winked at me.

Old Man Joe started to fight off the grasp, that I had on his arm.

"Let go of me, gal! You holding onto me for dear life. Stop squeezing my arm," he said.

"Grace, I got him," Big Tuna said and grabbed Old Man Joe under the arm, lifting his heels up a 1/2 inch off of the ground.

"Boy, you know what I told you about that?" Old man Joe scolded.

Big Tuna pushed Old Man Joe inside their apartment and slammed their door shut!

CHAPTER 17

Just as I was unlocking the door, David flung the door wide open.

"Hey, Grace. Can you drop me off at the mall?" he asked.

"David, I've been out all day. I'm exhausted," I said. "Besides, you haven't said two words to me in four months aside from, "hi, bye," and "give me some of that food that you're fixing.""

Surprisingly enough, David didn't have a smart comment, like he normally did.

"Is Franklin and Anna Mae still here?" I asked.

"YUP!" he said, sounding annoyed, "and it looks like they are not going anywhere, anytime soon. Anna Mae is in there now preparing a lasagna."

"So, why can't you ask Franklin to take you?" I asked.

"Nah. He's on the phone calling people to tell them that Momma died," he said.

"Oh," I said.

David didn't know that I was looking out the window the day that the cop pulled him over for the DUI, right out in front of the house. Lucky for him, the cop went to high school with Franklin, so he didn't have Momma's car towed but he sure did suspend David's license, to teach him a lesson.

"Oh yeah, Auntie Mabeline said that she will be here tomorrow," he said, "and she wants you to take her shopping to get a hat for Momma's funeral. So, good luck with that! I do not want to have no parts in going to no mall with ya'll tomorrow. That southern drawl of hers, drives me crazy!" he said.

David lied about a lot of stuff, but he was telling the truth about Auntie Mabeline. Auntie Mabeline was Momma's only sibling. She was three years younger than Momma and lived in Savannah, Georgia. She's been a school teacher, going on twenty years and would come up every summer to stay a month with Momma but she would drive the rest of us bananas.

"So, are you going to take me or what? We could have been halfway to the mall by now," he said. "Come on, Grace. I'll give you $20.00," David bribed.

It surprised me that David didn't have a job but he always seemed to have money in his pocket and was always decked out in a new outfit and the latest Air Jordan sneakers.

"Ok," I said, grabbing the $20.00. "You need to hurry up before I change my mind."

As we walked out of the house, into the hall way, an eerie feeling came over me. It was the strongest when I stood right near the storage closet. Too scared to look, I turned around and hurried downstairs.

"Hurry up David! Let's go!" I yelled up the stairs.

David flew down the steps and jumped in the passenger's seat. In his normal way, he laid the seat all the way back like a recliner.

"Who are you hiding from, David," I asked.

"Mind ya business and just drive. You ask way too many questions, Anna Mae Jr," he teased.

As we passed by the woman's house that helped me, it seemed very creepy and vacant.

"I wonder if they ever found out who killed that woman?" I said, looking at the house as I slowly drove past.

"Who knows. She was a weirdo," David said. Raising his head up, looking toward the house, from a reclined position.

Since David was in a talking mood, I decided to inquire, "So where are you getting all this money from David? Last I checked, you didn't have a job."

"I definitely ain't getting it from you," he said.

Once we arrived at the South Shore Plaza, I was just too tired to drop David off just, to come back to get him.

"How long are you going to be?" I asked, pulling up to Macy's so he could get out.

"Not long. Why? You gonna wait? I was up here yesterday. They holding some clothes for me, I'm just going to pay for them and be out. Give me 30 minutes," he said.

"David, I swear, if you are not out by 7:30pm on the dot, I'm leaving you," I said, looking at my watch.

"Hush. You ain't leaving nobody," David said as he wrestled with the car to get his big body out of it.

While waiting for him to return, I dozed off to sleep in the car until my ringing phone woke me out of my sleep.

"Hello," I said.

"Grace, where are you at, now?" Anna Mae asked.

"Anna Mae, just because I lost one mother, does not mean I need another. So please stop,!" I said.

"Anyways," she said. "Pastor Fallback called and he's coming over to the house later to give his condolences and to help us plan Momma's homegoing service," she said, "So you and that trifling brother of ours, wherever he disappeared to, need to be here. You two will not make me look foolish. You know what I'm sayin'?"

"First of all, Anna Mae, I'm with David at the mall. Second of all, we don't have to make you look anything that you already are. Third of all, why are you still saying, "you know what I'm saying?" I thought you dropped that in your "Valley Girl," days," I challenged her.

CLICK.

Anna Mae hung up on me again.

"Ok bye," I said, as I rolled my eyes.

"Where is this boy at," I said looking at the clock that read, 7:28 pm?

I looked up, to see David walking out of the mall, weighed down with bags from Abercrombie & Fitch, Macy's, J. Crew and The North Face with a woman that I had never seen before.

She was taller than David and looked to be in her early 40's. She was brown skinned, with long auburn colored, micro braids. She had on a pair of fitted dark blue jeans, with knee boots, a long sleeve white shirt, and a beige Mohair vest. She was holding as many bags, as David was. I watched them as they both walked over to her car. She tossed the Coach, Bebe, Charlotte Russe, Macy's and Nordstrom bags into the backseat of her red BMW convertible, with beige leather seats. She giggled before she gave David a peck on his cheek and mouthed, "thank you," to him.

I thought to myself, what on earth, did she see in a 21-year-old bum who didn't have a job. Either David is her boy toy, her pimp or he robbed a bank! David didn't say a word to me, as he opened the back door, putting his bags on the back seat, before sitting in the front. He was so different than he had been on our ride to the mall. The silence in the car between me and David was deafening. I could hear the music blasting out of David's earphones. He reclined back in the seat, with his eyes closed and his hands folded on his stomach. I didn't say anything to David about the woman or all of the new stuff that he had purchased. I was curious as to why David didn't have the woman drop him off at the house. I didn't dare ask. I'm sure she knew where we lived at. I figured that the woman is probably who he had been spending time with, for the past four months. It infuriated me to think, that David could be so selfish, to leave me at home, by myself to cope with Momma being in a coma for months, while he just lived his life, acting like it didn't faze him. David remained in the same position until I pulled up in from of our apartment.

CHAPTER 18

——————

Pastor Fallback's shiny, black, Cadillac Escalade, with the gold rims was parked out front. I never could understand, why a man who stood five feet tall, would drive a car that was too big for him. David let out a big sigh, as he opened his eyes, noticing the Cadillac. "Now I gotta deal with this old "shucking and jiving" dude," he said. I didn't know what he dreaded most, seeing Pastor Fallback or planning Momma's funeral.

I got out of the car, not commenting on what David said. I closed the door putting my Ivy Cross bag over my body. David had rolled himself out of the passenger's side.

"Yo. Grace, pop the trunk?" he asked, as he gathered up all of his shopping bags from the backseat.

"Why David?" I said, knowing that he didn't want Franklin or Anna Mae to ask him the same questions that I had in my mind, about his shopping spree, knowing he had no job and zero income coming in, that we knew of.

"Did I ask you, why you went out the house with your hair looking like you stuck your finger in a plug socket?" he asked. "Just pop the trunk."

I was in no mood to argue with David or for his corny jokes. That's all David ever talked about, was my hair. He used to tell me that when I have kids, that is the only thing that they would have going for them, inheriting my "good hair," as he called it. If he was not making fun of it, he was pulling on it. Out of all of Momma's kids, I was the only one that had thick, naturally curly hair. He was just mad because he kept a head full of naps. I popped the trunk and headed upstairs.

The stairs leading to our apartment, creeped me out, for two reasons. The image played over and over in my head of the EMT's carrying Momma down the same flight of stairs that the perpetrator dragged me down. I was so glad that Franklin was able to get leave from the Army and had decided to stay with us for a few days, until after Momma's funeral. I was even more thrilled that he finally snapped out of the spell that Anna Mae had him under. I passed Old Man Joe's apartment door, heading upstairs when Big Tuna flung open the door as if he was trying to catch me.

"Hey Shorty," he said. I caught him looking at my butt like I was a pork chop as I walked up the steps.

"Hi," I said, nervously.

"You look like you're in a rush. Stop down later. I got something to give you," he said.

I don't know what Big Tuna wanted to give me, unless he saw his father trying to give me ten dollars in food stamps, in exchange for bringing him on errands. I had no intentions of going back downstairs and the way that Big Tuna had been looking at me in recent months, gave me the heebie jeebies.

When I reached the top of the stairs, I could hear David having words with Big Tuna. I stayed silent, listening to their heated exchange.

"Man, I saw how you looked at my little sister. I advise that you keep your eyes in your head." I could hear David saying.

"Bro, It's a free country. I am free to do what I want and that includes looking at your sister, who's not so little," Big Tuna said.

"Just remember what I said," David said. He took his sweet time coming up the stairs. He stopped and looked down near Big Tuna's direction and said, "…and I'm not your bro!"

CHAPTER 19

I opened the door before David could catch up to me. Pastor fallback had his back toward me, as I walked in. He had just arrived. He shook Franklin's hand, as Anna Mae stood beside him, holding a box of Kleenex.

"It's good to see you, under the circumstances. You know your Momma was so proud of you," Pastor Fallback said, shaking Franklin's hand. "Thank you for your service to this country. I don't need to tell you all, how fine of a woman Ms. Leola was," he said. Holding his fedora over his heart, looking at all of us.

"Thank you, sir. Yes, she was," Franklin said, nodding his head in agreement. He stood there looking like the epitome of strength.

Pastor Fallback looked Franklin up and down, with his chest poked out, in such contrast to Franklin's majestic body. "Franklin, you've grown into a fine young man. We are going to have to find you a nice young woman, who can throw down in the kitchen just like Sister Leola. We got a few wholesome ones, down at the church," Pastor Fallback said, trying to lighten the mood.

"Okay," Franklin chuckled.

Anna Mae cleared her throat as if to alert Pastor Fallback of her presence. At which time Pastor Fallback looked up at her and smiled.

"Anna Mae, come on over here, girl," Pastor Fallback said, hugging Anna Mae so tight that her breasts cupped his chin, as she towered over him.

"You done went off and got married on me. Oh! I meant on us," he quickly corrected himself, as he chuckled. "Where's that husband of yours? When am, I going to meet him?" Pastor Fallback said, looking around.

"He works a lot, Pastor. You know what I'm saying?" Anna Mae said.

"No. I don't," Pastor Fallback said. "Anna Mae," he said, peering over his glasses, "looks like you and I need to sit down and have a chat. Call down to the church in about a week and let's set up an appointment," Pastor Fallback said. Clearly, he was reading between the lines that everyone could see but Anna Mae.

"Okay," Anna Mae said grinning as if she had been dunked in some blonde rinse. What he said flew right over her head like the bird who flew over the cuckoo's nest.

I walked up to Pastor Fallback and gave him a hug, leaving a foot of space between us, so he wouldn't feel my baby bump.

"There's my amazing, Grace," he said. He leaned back, looking me up and down with his eyes.

"Hi, Pastor Fallback," I said.

"It's about time you started putting some meat on them bones of yours," he said as if he knew my secret. "Look at you, just as adorable as you want to be. Looking just like that Braxton girl. You know the one that made all that money," he said. "Toni," I said, "Yeah. I get that all the time," replying with a light smile. I stood in front of him with my orange ruched tank dress. It was one of my outfits that hid my small baby bump well. Topped with a cropped jean jacket and my favorite coach sandals.

"Thank you for coming," I said.

"Aww baby girl, it's my job to be there for the bereaved. I'm so sorry for the loss of your Momma. Now, Sister Leola loved her baby girl. You were so dedicated to your Momma, driving her down to the church after she got sick and couldn't drive herself. The Lord is gonna bless ya!" He said placing his hand on my forehead as if I was about to get baptized and he was ready to dunk me in the water.

Pastor Fallback pulled me in for another hug. My eyes must have spoken what my mouth couldn't speak; I needed another hug. Suddenly something came over Anna Mae as if she was looking for attention. "I MISS MY MOMMA," she wailed.

Pastor Fallback let go of me and rushed back over to Anna Mae. He held both of her hands, looking eye level straight into her plump breasts, that looked more like two bronze golden globes.

"Aww, now baby. Your momma is in a better place," Pastor Fallback said, "You gonna have to hold on to the memories that you had of her. So, when was the last time that you visited her?" he asked, looking up, into Anna Mae's eyes.

It was as if Pastor Fallback had struck a nerve.

"Oh, there's David," Anna Mae shouted; abruptly taking the focus off of her.

Pastor Fallback turned around to greet David.

"David, man, how are you doing? I cannot remember the last time I've seen you. I wouldn't have been able to pick you up out of a lineup, it's been so long. You doing alright?" he asked, shaking David's hand and pulling him in for a half of a hug.

David, not even making eye contact with Pastor Fallback said, "Yeah. I'm hanging in there,"

"That's what your Momma would want you to do," Pastor Fallback replied.

"Well, let's all sit down and discuss your Momma's home going celebration,"

Me, David and Franklin sat on the couch. Anna Mae squeezed her wide hips on the love seat right next to Pastor Fallback

"Pastor Fallback, can I fix you something to eat? I made some lasagna," Anna Mae said enticingly. "You better get it now before these two greedy guts eat it all up," she said, looking at me and David.

"Bless your heart, Anna Mae. I'm too full now but I'll take some to go. First Lady done filled me up off them toasted cheese sandwiches that she makes. I'm feeling a little backed up now, so it's best that I don't eat any more dairy," Pastor Fallback said. He shared way more information than any of us cared to know.

"Well, I'll go wrap you some up now before Grace and David get to it," Anna Mae said as she stood up to walk towards the kitchen.

Before she could finish her strut, all of a sudden David raised his voice and blurted out, "ANNA MAE, WHY ARE YOU EVEN HERE? WHEN WAS THE LAST TIME THAT YOU CAME TO SEE YOUR MOMMA? WHY ARE YOU TRYING TO ACT LIKE YOU ARE SO CONCERNED NOW THAT SHE'S DEAD!"

The room had come to a piercing silence. We were all shocked, even though David was right! I had never seen David so agitated. He and Anna Mae had gotten into it many times before but never in front of company.

"Well. Maybe we should have opened up with a little prayer," Pastor Fallback said attempting to calm David down.

David continued, "I DON'T NEED PRAYER PASTOR. SHE NEEDS A REALITY CHECK. SHE THINKS SHE'S SO HIGH AND MIGHTY, LIKE HER SH..." Franklin cut David off.

"STOP DAVID!" Franklin said as he stood up. "Now, I know that we are all feeling the loss of Momma but she definitely would not want us to act like this. We have to remember how Momma raised us, with good morals and values," Franklin said, "We gotta keep it together!"

Anna Mae stopped, placing her hands on her hip as she looked at David, and proceeded into the kitchen without saying a word.

I sat there quiet as a church mouse. For some reason, it seemed as if, something more than Momma's death was bothering David. I wondered if it had to do with that woman at the mall?

"Franklin is right," Pastor Fallback said, as he stood up as if he was about to preach a sermon, loosening his paisley green tie.

"Sorry Pastor," David said, regaining his composure.

After two hours of sitting with Pastor Fallback, we finally finished the program for Momma's homegoing service. Franklin agreed to call the funeral home to make sure that we were all on the same page.

David and Anna Mae seemed to have called a truce, for the time being, both offering to take part in Momma's program.

Anna Mae volunteered to read Momma's obituary, after insulting Auntie Mabeline, who had told Anna Mae over the phone earlier, that she wanted to read it.

Anna Mae said that Auntie Mabeline talks too slow and that she would put the entire church to sleep. If there was one thing that she and David agreed on without the need to cuss each other out, that was it!

David agreed to sing Momma's favorite song, "Precious Lord." That's one thing that Momma loved to hear him do. It's too bad it was a pity that she wouldn't be here to hear him serenade her.

Pastor Fallback sat on the edge of the couch, looking like he swallowed a canary.

"I wanted to also come by and have a conversation with the four of you," he said hesitantly clearing his throat.

We looked at each other, perplexed as to what else Pastor Fallback had to say.

"You know the last time we had your extended family at the church for the choir celebration, they brought their own aluminum foil and packed up all of the food before we could feed the guests. Some of your people said that, Sis. Leola cooked the food and she always said, "take care of your family first." Now, I know they took that totally out of context because I know that's not what Sis. Leola meant" Pastor Fallback said, wiping the sweat beads from his forehead.

David laughed, "So, you want us to make sure that they don't come and act ghetto. Is that what you're trying to say?"

Pastor Fallback pushed his glasses back up on his nose and continued, "Well no. Well, I guess yeah," he said, sounding confused. "I just want to let you know, so that it doesn't come to you as a surprise, that I'm gonna have some of the deacons on guard, so this type of behavior doesn't happen at your Momma's repast. I cannot have Ms. Leola rolling in her grave, haunting me in my sleep" he said.

"With that being said, I'm gonna apologize now. Since there's not enough money in the bereavement fund, the diaconate board decided that they are going to order a couple buckets of chicken, some string beans, and some dirty rice, from the Chicken Shack, down there on Crawford Street. They don't want their food to be compared to Ms. Leola's."

"Hear me out now," Pastor Fall back continued, "Now, ya'll already know, no one can place a match to your Momma's cooking. Sister Leola could burn in the kitchen! That homemade soup she made for the homeless folks, had many of them lining up for seconds," he said, attempting to crack a smile.

Pastor Fallback was right. I guess we had been spoiled, taking Momma's and her skills in the kitchen, for granted. We really didn't appreciate just how good of a cook she really was. Momma could go in the kitchen and whip up a meal out of scraps, that would have you licking the bowl. Pastor Fallback started wiping his brow, "So, once we get back from the burial site, don't ya'll tarry, get downstairs and eat first, just in case there is a shortage of food."

Pastor Fallback tried to make light of the situation, "Well, maybe I can have First Lady put together some of them tuna fish sandwiches and cold cuts that she makes." Showing his gold shiny tooth, he smiled and said, "I don't think you want First Lady down there cooking. Ya'll may get sick. That's why I'm so thin," he laughed, as he held his hand against his $2,000.00 Giorgio Armani navy blue suit.

I looked at Franklin, who clearly looked pissed off. I imagined that he was probably thinking the same thing that I was. After all of the sacrifices that Momma made for the church, this was not the time to discuss how jealous the woman was of Momma's cooking or tell us about a sorry store bought meal.

"Wow," David said, as he shook his head in disbelief of what Pastor Fallback was saying. He looked at me, attempting to place me in the tangled web that he was about to weave, "What did I say earlier Grace? Shucking and jiving".

I ignored David, pretending as if I didn't hear him.

"This is some bull," David said under his breath, shaking his head.

Before David "set it off" yet again, Franklin redirected the conversation, before it turned ugly. Franklin looking at Anna Mae who sat there, oddly enough, in silence said, "So why don't you have someone from the diaconate board call Anna Mae on tomorrow to see if we can work something out?"

"It's getting late Pastor Fallback. We appreciate you coming by."

Franklin walked over to the door and opened it. It was a subtle way of telling Pastor Fallback, "You ain't gotta go home but you gotta get the hell up out of here!"

CHAPTER 20

The next morning, I woke up to the sound of a blaring smoke alarm. I jumped up out of the bed and put my fluffy robe on; surprised that it could still stretch over my growing stomach. My morning sickness had subsided and I didn't feel as nauseous as I had been. I stuck my feet into my sheepskin bed slippers and walked straight toward the unfamiliar sound.

"Franklin what are you doing? Burning down the kitchen?" I said, jokingly, as I watched Franklin sit the smoky pot of grits in the sink.

I opened the door to the pantry and grabbed the folded step ladder. I opened it up directly under the smoke detector, as I climbed up on it and removed the battery.

"Good morning lil' sis," he said. "I was in here trying to chef it up and looks like I am failing miserably," Franklin said laughing, as the steam from the pot of burnt grits covered his face as if he was giving himself a facial.

"Yeah, I would have to agree with you there," I said, giggling, climbing down from the step ladder and walking over to the see-through kitchen cabinet where Momma kept the mugs.

"I didn't mean to wake you," he said.

"Oh, I was up. Lately, I've been a light sleeper. That's the difference between me and David," I said.

It was odd seeing Franklin out of his Army uniform. It had been a long time since I'd seen him dressed down. He had on a white tank top, red and black plaid pajama bottoms and Nike slippers and his usual; striped tube socks. His muscles were on fleek.

"Waking up in Momma's house, without the sweet smell of a hot breakfast, just feels weird to me" he said. "I miss hearing the sizzling sound of that hickory smoked bacon, Momma used to cook," he said.

"I know," I said, somberly.

"And she loved making me my favorite; homemade biscuits and gravy," he said, licking his lips.

"Yeah. We all had a favorite dish that Momma made," I said. "Mine was fried chicken and homemade waffles, with blueberries," I said, rubbing my stomach. "Delish!"

"Mmmh. Now that sounds good right about now" Franklin said. "Momma loved to cook and I love to eat, especially when she tried a new recipe. So, I thought I'd try my skills at making something new and surprise you and David" he said.

"What were you trying to make?" I asked, removing my red and black polka dot tea cup from the cabinet and sitting it on the counter.

"Well, since I burnt part of the surprise, I guess I can tell you" Franklin said. "I was attempting to make a southern grits casserole, with egg, sausage, and cheese," he said.

I gagged, "I'll take whatever is behind cabinet door number 1," I said as we laughed. "Well, that's if David didn't get to it already," I added, with a sigh.

Franklin nodded and smirked, in agreement.

"That fool will eat the last of something and leave the empty container in the cabinet," I said, shaking my head. "That irks me."

"Speaking of David," Franklin said, reaching for the unopened box of pancakes, that were in the cabinet "is he okay? Yesterday, he was acting a bit strange. I know he has always been Momma's problem child but I don't know if it's the loss of Momma that has him feeling a certain kind of way and that's why he's acting out or what? But the way he went in on Anna Mae, man oh man," Franklin said, shaking his head like he was surprised, "I've never seen him that angry."

I sat at the table, looking down, playing with a napkin, folding it ten times, wondering if I should tell Franklin about what happened to me, the day that Momma fell and I was sexually assaulted. And how I blamed David for carelessly leaving the door open. I also wanted to tell Franklin how David had been staying out of the house, more than he'd been home, ever since Momma's fall and about the shopping spree that David went on with the unknown older woman and that he'd been decked out for the past few months in new clothes and shoes, when we all knew that he didn't have a job. Was he a drug dealer? Was he a pimp? I wanted to tell Franklin everything. Since Franklin bought it up and David was still asleep, I felt like this was my chance to finally let out what I'd been holding onto for months.

"Well, the day Momma...." I stopped mid-sentence, catching the sight of David's white socks, as he stood in the doorway of the kitchen, staring me down.

"So, what are ya'll talking about?" David asked with his arms folded looking straight at me as if I was in trouble.

Franklin hadn't realized that David had been standing in the doorway, either. "Hey man. We are talking about you! What's going on with you? You went in on Anna Mae last night like I had never seen before," Franklin said, not holding back any punches, picking up the pan, tossing the pancake up in the air, back into the pan.

"Stuff," David said.

"Well, what kind of stuff bro," Franklin asked. "Man, you know if you need to talk, I'm here. And that goes for you too Grace. I know that Momma's loss directly impacts the both of you, more than me and Anna Mae because you both live here. Me and Anna Mae spoke and we are going to do all we can to keep this place. Momma worked so hard after Daddy's death, to keep us afloat and with Old Man Joe's income from section 8, steadily coming in, I don't see any reason for us to sell. So, if that's your worry, don't worry about that. We got you!"

I don't know about David, but with everything else going on the thought did cross my mind during the past four months. I overheard Franklin, a few months back, ask Anna Mae on the phone to keep him in the loop of what was going on but I didn't realize that she would actually listened to him, for a change. I felt relieved knowing that he was working with Anna Mae on keeping Momma's bills up, but hearing Franklin say it, made me feel better since Anna Mae was being so secretive towards me about it.

David seemed as if he was not concerned with whatever Franklin said. I started to feel some tension, or jealously. We all knew that Momma favored Franklin, as the oldest, just as much as she spoiled me, as the youngest. So, David has always felt some kind of way, toward the both of us, even though Momma spent more time dealing with him and his foolishness. With Anna Mae, she was always caught up in her own world. Momma just let her be.

"There's one more thing," Franklin said.

"What's that?" I said.

David stood there in silence as if he was waiting for the other shoe to drop.

"Well, I don't know how you two are going to feel about this but Anna Mae suggested that maybe she and Rufus should move back here," he said looking intently to see our expression.

"Aww, hell to the naw!" David exclaimed.

"What he said," I said, pointing to David, in agreement.

Just when we needed something to cut the tension, the house phone rang.

"I got it," I said getting up from the table, as David left the kitchen.

"Hello?" I answered.

"Just the person who I wanted to speak to," Anna Mae said.

"Hi Anna Mae, what's up?" I said not even mentioning what Franklin just shared with us.

"I hope ya'll are not over there working Franklin's nerves," she said. I rolled my eyes, as I thought about what Momma would say to me, when I use to do that. She would look at me and say, "Grace, one day them eyes of yours are going to get stuck up there." But whenever I spoke to Anna Mae, I took my chances.

"Grace, Rufus is going to drop me off on Friday, so that we can walk to Misty's Salon, and get our hair done before Momma's funeral on Saturday. If I'm going to get my hair done, I'd rather go to Misty so she can hook this sister up. Plus, it's been a minute since I've seen her. It will be good to catch up," Anna Mae said, sounding as if she was having a conversation by herself.

"Ok, but I can only get a press and curl," I said. I caught the slip of my tongue, right before I almost revealed my secret. But it went right over Anna Mae's head; she didn't notice a thing.

"Oh, that reminds me," she said, "I have to talk to her when we get there and ask her if she can go to the funeral home and do Momma's hair. I cannot trust Franklin to take care of something that important," she said, "and you know Momma don't want no hands in her hair, dead or alive, unless its Misty's."

Anna Mae was right about that. Momma had mentioned to me, way before she had gotten really sick, that she wanted no one but Misty to do her hair, if God took her away from this earth. Momma trusted Misty. I reflected back on yesterday, when I ran into Misty at the pharmacy. She gave me her word that she would not share my pregnancy. I believed her.

"Hold on, while I call the hair salon on three way, so we can set up an appointment," Anna Mae said. "Lord knows, you can't be going to Momma's funeral following behind me looking like, "who done it and ran" with all that wild hair of yours."

Ana Mae always had a way of hurling insults at me, while making it all about herself. Before I could say anything, Anna Mae connected the three-way call and Misty's answering service for the hair salon came on. I recognized Kia's voice. She was the pleasant receptionist, who greeted me when I was last there. Her voice sounded smooth as silk.

"Hello, you have reached Misty's Mane Cuts. We are a unisex shop, where we specialize in braids, fades, weaves and more. Please leave your name and number so that we can call you back to schedule an appointment. Remember, you are too blessed, to not have your naps pressed."

BEEEEP.

Anna Mae, trying to sound all prim and proper said, "Hi, this is Anna Mae. Ya'll know who I am. I'm Ms. Leola's oldest daughter. The beautiful one," as she chuckled in a phony kind of way: almost as if she didn't believe her own statement.

I stood there, leaning against the wall, rolling my eyes at Anna Mae's need for attention, since Rufus obviously wasn't giving it to her. She continued, "I need to set up an appointment for me and my sister Grace for this coming Friday," Anna Mae cleared her throat, as if a frog was stuck in it, adding, "Misty is the only one who does my hair. My sister Grace, will see that girl Vonda. She's just getting a press and curl. Ya'll may need a steamroller to get her curls straight," Anna Mae laughed then added, "I know ya'll have caller ID. So, call me back. Thank you! Bye!"

I was furious at Anna Mae. It wasn't enough that I had just lost the only woman who had been there for me but you would think that of all people, she would understand, that if she wasn't there for me before, now would be a good time. I picked up where David left off last night during our meeting with Pastor Fallback.

"Anna Mae!" I said, letting her hear in my voice, that I was angry. "You know that I don't like that girl touching my head! The last time I went to her, she had my forehead burnt like a crispy piece of bacon and Momma had to put Crisco on my burns. Plus, her own hair always looks jacked up!"

Anna Mae fell out laughing on the other end of the phone, "Lord child, you are funny," she said, then attempting to be serious. "Grace, get over yourself! That was a while ago. I'm sure, if she's still there, she's gotten a lot of practice in since then."

"Then, Anna Mae, you go to her and let her singe your forehead!"

All of a sudden, we heard, "BEEEEEP!"

Anna Mae hadn't disconnected from the three-way call.

"Oooops!" Anna Mae said, as she laughed hysterically. "Well, I guess now, they'll know how you really feel!

Vonda's really gonna jack your head up now!"

I slammed the phone down on the hook.

CHAPTER 21

"She makes me so sick!" I said, not realizing that Franklin heard me.

"You must be talking about Anna Mae. If you keep letting her get to you, you are going to be popping blood pressure medication just like Auntie Mabeline," he said.

I leaned against the doorframe, with my hands resting on my little baby bump. Discreetly looking down closing my robe and folding my arms, as I watched Franklin water Momma's plants in the kitchen, that I'd pretty much neglected for months.

"Oh, by the way, Auntie Mabeline's flight gets in at 3:00 pm today. Do you want to go with me to get her?" he asked.

"Yeah, I'll go," I said. "I'm kind of looking forward to seeing her. She reminds me so much of Momma. It'll be like having Momma here again."

"Yeah, I agree! I'm trying to deal with the loss of Momma too, but the other night when me and Anna Mae called her, she took Momma's death so hard, she was hollering on the phone, then she started reminiscing, all the way back to their childhood, up to their adulthood. By the time we looked up at the clock, three hours had gone by!" he said.

"Well, we are all grieving Momma's loss in our own way," I said.

"I know," Franklin said, as he looked at me in my eyes and through to my heart. "I've been impressed by you, Grace,"

"Why you say that," I asked.

"We all had our special relationship with Momma but you were the closest to her. When Anna Mae broke down yesterday, while Pastor Fallback was here, I was looking at you, making sure that you were okay. I thought that you'd be next. But you were strong," he said.

My lip started to quiver, noticing Momma's favorite apron hanging on the wall, that still held her scent. "Well, I have been here helping Momma and quite frankly, there were so many days that I had to be strong. Seeing the pain in Momma's eyes from the cancer, when she would struggle just to get out of bed, killed me on the inside," I said, wiping my eyes. "I guess I have a clear conscience, unlike some people," I said, throwing shade at Anna Mae, not realizing that I may have offended Franklin in the process. Franklin sat the silver watering can on the windowsill. He walked over toward me, swallowing me up in his large frame and gave me a bear hug. "Thank you for being there for Momma," he said, resting his chin on the top of my head before he gingerly let me go.

Feeling the warmth of Franklin's hug, made me feel liberated, as I continued sharing my running thoughts.

"The day of Momma's fall, I was in here cooking breakfast, so David went to help her. Sometimes I wonder if I went and helped her instead, would she still be here? As for Anna Mae, the last time we saw her was about a year ago. I think that's why David was so upset at her. She'd stopped coming by and only called Momma to complain about Rufus. So, all them crocodile tears of hers, have guilt written all of over them," I added. "Even with David being as lazy as he is, he'd give me a hard time but he would help out some."

Franklin looked as if he shared some of Anna Mae's guilt, "Yeah, I wish I had called Momma more or tried to get leave to come see about her more often."

Our mood had turned somber, so I changed the subject. "Did you eat up all the pancakes from us?" I said as I looked around, not a morsel to be found.

The short time that I'd been on the phone with Anna Mae, Franklin had cooked a stack of twelve pancakes, woofed down his share, and had cleaned up the kitchen. The Army had trained him well. Momma would be proud!

"I put the rest of the pancakes in the microwave for you and David," Franklin said. "But I heard David leave out. I guess, I must've pissed him off now, so the pancakes are all yours."

"Right about now, I don't even want to talk about David, from the dirty look that he gave me, when I was sitting at the table earlier," I said.

"Yeah, I caught that," Franklin said. "But as long as I am here, you let me worry about David, okay?" he said, looking at me.

As strong as Franklin was, I pitied anyone who was on the other end of David's rage. I stood up from the table.

"Okay. I'll eat after I get dressed," I said and walked away with my head down as if I had lost my best friend.

"Grace?" he called out. "I know you probably don't want to hear this but Anna Mae plans to come over later tonight to see Auntie Mabeline and to make some pies for Momma's funeral tomorrow. She may need your help," he said.

"I'll help......for Momma," I said.

"One more thing," he said. "She mentioned that the both of you will need to go through Momma's closet to see what can be donated. It doesn't have to be any time soon since the loss of Momma is so raw for all of us, but I just want to let you know," he said.

"Since she told you, Franklin, please tell her don't bother. I got it!" I said. "I would kill myself, if I had to be stuck in Momma's closet all day with her," I pretended to hang myself with an invisible rope.

Franklin and I both laughed.

"I'll be ready by 2!" I said.

"Okay, lil' sis," he said with a warm smile.

"Franklin?" I said as I stopped with my hand on the door frame.

"What's up," he asked.

"I'm glad you are here," I said.

Franklin smiled and I went to get dressed.

CHAPTER 22

"Grace, are you ready?" Franklin yelled.

"Yes! I'm coming," I hollered back. I was looking forward to seeing Auntie Mabeline. Even though she would get on our nerves, having her here would be just like having Momma around.

I looked at myself in the mirror, making sure that I camouflaged my stomach. My jean popover dress seemed to do the trick. I put on my navy-blue sweater with my red cross over bag and stuck my feet inside my red, white and blue Old Navy flip flops. I picked up the can of Motions Oil Sheen & Conditioning and sprayed it liberally across my dark brown flat ironed hair.

"You look good Grace," I said, talking to myself in the mirror.

"Grace, we have to get going," Franklin yelled.

"I'm coming," I said, reaching into the closet, feeling for the coat, that I hid my money in.

I had been out of work for so long, tending to Momma, that my only reminder that I was still on the payroll at the bank, was the money that I had stashed away from my paid vacation and sick time that I had accrued. My boss had been so understanding when I told him of Momma's fall and then of her passing. But he did say that once I came back, we needed to talk. I'm sure he was ready to let me go but there had been so much sadness in the past few months, that I couldn't let that bother me or get me down. As Momma used to say, "the Lord will make a way somehow." Plus, the thought of seeing Auntie Mabeline put me in a better mood.

Since we didn't hit any traffic, we arrived at the airport in no time.

Franklin drove up into JetBlue's terminal C, for arrivals.

"Do you see her, Grace?" he asked.

"No. Not yet," I said taking my seatbelt off to get a better look.

The double doors opened up and this woman came walking out, shaped like a Christmas tree, looking just like the colors in a crayon box. She had on a straw fishing hat, with a hot pink feather on the side, a lime green blazer with a striped blue and pink Izod shirt under it, that she accessorized with purple oversized beads, that looked more like a choker, high-water jeans, and a pair of burgundy Keds.

"What in the world?" I said, laughing at what Auntie Mabeline had on. "There she is Franklin" I pointed.

"I don't get it," I said, shaking my head in disbelief, "Auntie Mabeline don't have a child or a chick. I don't understand why she can't put herself together better than she does."

Franklin was looking around as if he couldn't see Auntie Mabeline walking towards us looking like rainbow bright.

Auntie Mabeline sure didn't dress like Momma but she favored Momma in every other way. She stood 5'7' and weighed about 200lbs. She had a cute round face, with a mole below her right eye, high cheekbones, and flawless cocoa brown skin. Both of their hair was shoulder length, with a silvery gray tone. Unlike Momma, Auntie Mabeline had a donkey booty for days. Momma told me that's who I got my little round, shapely booty from.

"Where is she?" Franklin said.

"She's over there," I responded. "She's the one that looks like a bag of skittles."

We laughed.

"Now, be nice Grace," Franklin said.

"I know once Anna Mae sees her, with her Gucci wearing self, she is going to turn into the fashion police for real!" I said, giggling.

"Well, you know your sister thinks she's a fashion expert," he commented. "Grace, go get her before I get a ticket," he said looking in his side view mirror for the state troopers, who make sure that you don't stay parked too long in front of the entrance.

I reluctantly got out of the front seat and waved so that she could see me.

"Auntie Mabeline, we are over here," I said, as I walked toward her to greet her.

"Gracie, baby how you doing?" Auntie Mabeline asked. She put down her zebra print suitcase and gave me a big warm hug. She was the only one in our family who called me Gracie.

"I'm good," I said, feeling safe in her arms. "Do you want me to carry your suitcase?" I asked reaching for the handle. I picked up her luggage that seemed as if it weighed a ton, and immediately dropped it, feeling pressure in my stomach.

"OH! Auntie, this is too heavy for me," I said.

"Chile, I'm gonna have to feed you some chicken liver, garlic, and onions, while I'm up here," she said. "You need some iron in that body of yours."

"I'm so sorry for the loss of your Momma," she said as we walked toward the car.

"Chile, I miss your Momma so bad, that I cried all the way here, on that plane. I 'bout near cleared out the two rows of passengers in front of me. The little stewardess, with the bad breath, came over telling me that she was going to move my seat. That little chicken head moved me all the way to the back, near the bathroom. Then, if that wasn't bad enough, one of them passengers went in there. Lord, I don't know if he had a bad batch of chitterlings but he cleared them stewardess straight out that back, leaving me there to fend for myself. I had to use my wool scarf your Momma gave me, to cover my mouth and my nose.

Then chile, I started crying again, smelling your Momma's sweet perfume on the scarf," she said.

Auntie Mabeline started stripping, removing the lime green jacket that she was wearing. "Lord chile, this cool Boston air feels good. It may get my arthritis out of whack but it will be good for my hot flashes. The pilot didn't know what he was talking about neither. He said it was 60 something degrees here. I'll take this cool weather any day, especially over them blizzards that ya'll get. Especially for November," she said. Auntie Mabeline clearly did not understand New England's unpredictable weather.

Auntie Mabeline stopped, dropping her suitcase to the ground, looking at me, breaking my concentration. I should have known better, since she was a school teacher that she was onto me, noticing that I'd stepped over every crack in the pavement, that we passed by, as I played the game in my head, "step on a crack, break your mother's back."

"Chile, you working my nerves already. Just stop it! She exclaimed. "Act like a young lady with good sense. Show some etiquette and stop walking beside me, looking like an untrained Clydesdale horse," she said. "Now, head up and posture straight. You know you're Momma taught you better than that. She didn't name you Grace for nothing," she bent at her knees, lifting her suitcase up, off of the ground.

I had no words, as I walked with poise beside Auntie Mabeline thinking, Franklin owes me big!

CHAPTER 23

"Franklin, I like this car. What kind of car is this?" Auntie Mabeline asked, gliding her hand across the dashboard.

"It's an Infiniti," Franklin said.

"Chile, you doing alright for yourself, I see," Auntie Mabeline said rubbing on the black leather seats.

Franklin laughed, "Yeah. Momma raised me well."

As Franklin turned onto our dead-end street, the police cruiser passed by in the opposite direction.

"Yes, she did," Auntie Mabeline said. "She raised you to work hard and buy your own sh...." I cut Auntie Mabeline off, in mid-sentence. She saved her firestorm of curse words for the summer since she couldn't swear at her students. "Oh, my God!" I said. "Looks like they arrested Big Tuna!"

"Lord, chile, where ya'll bringing me to, a war zone?" Auntie Mabeline asked, not even paying attention to Big Tuna but noticing the faded yellow tape, blowing off the banister of the house that the woman was murdered at.

"Naw, Auntie Mabeline. That's Old Man Joe's son. He was in the pen the last time you were here" Franklin said. "I don't talk to that dude, outside of saying, "hi and bye." Momma had told Old Man Joe that he didn't want him staying with him but Old Man Joe can't remember much nowadays and just continues to let him back in. I had mentioned to her, to let me know if she needed me to come and ask Big Tuna to leave, but she never did."

Auntie Mabeline looked in the side view mirror, as the police car turned the corner and was out of her sight.

"Poor critter," Auntie Mabeline said referring to Old Man Joe. "I think I have some of that Milk of Magnesium in my suitcase and some Ginkgo Biloba. I reckon I can pinch some off and give it to him" she said.

"Isn't Milk of Magnesium for constipation?" Franklin asked.

"Yeah," Auntie Mabeline said. "But he may be backed up, with his little ole' self and it's messing with his mind. But the Ginkgo should help him with his memory," she said.

"I don't know about all that," Franklin said, as he backed into the parking spot. "Unless you came with a miracle pill," he chuckled. As Auntie Mabeline and Franklin spoke, I sat in the backseat quiet, wondering what Big Tuna had done.

"Well, I hope his son isn't in too much trouble for Old Man Joe's sake. He seems to really depend on him," Franklin said, turning the car off.

"Well, that father of his is something else. Your Momma used to say, "Mabeline, stop talking to that nasty man before he tries to feel on that booty of yours,"" Auntie Mabeline laughed.

Franklin opened his car door.

"Okay. The eagle has landed," he smiled. "I'll get your luggage. You and Grace can head on upstairs," Franklin said.

Me and Auntie Mabeline got out of the car and started walking up the few steps, leading to the porch. When we got into the hallway, Auntie Mabeline stopped.

"Chile, you go ahead upstairs. I'm going to check on Old Man Joe. Let him know I'm back in town," she said.

I gave Auntie Mabeline a look, thinking back on what she just shared in the car and then headed upstairs.

Two hours later, while me and Franklin was in the kitchen checking to see what ingredients Anna Mae needed to make the pies, Auntie Mabeline came walking into the kitchen. Auntie Mabeline sat down at the kitchen table, out of breath, like she had just run a marathon.

"Oooh chile, them stairs are a killer," she said. "What are you two doing?"

Franklin took his head out of the refrigerator and I took my head out of the cabinet and we both looked at Auntie Mabeline, unable to hide our shocked expression.

Her hair looked as if it was blowing in the wind. Her striped shirt was buttoned all wrong and her purple beaded necklace was missing from around her neck.

Franklin stood up with a grin on his face, "So how's Old Man Joe doing?"

Auntie Mabeline looked as if she was a kid, caught with her hand in the cookie jar.

"He fine. He fine," she said. "He was happy that I came to sit with him."

"I bet he was," Franklin said, smirking.

"So, what did he say Big Tuna got arrested for?" I asked.

"Oh, chile. I didn't ask him about that. I had forgotten all about that," she said.

"So, Auntie Mabeline, you been down there for two hours and you didn't even ask the man what happened to his son and why the cops had taken him away. So, what were ya'll doing?" Franklin asked, grinning, sounding more like curious George.

"Boy, I know you are grown, but you need to stay out of old folk's business," she said.

"Auntie Mabeline," I exclaimed.

Auntie Mabeline looked at me, as if her eyes said, "Don't start with me, lil' Gracie."

"What chile?" she said, seemingly agitated.

"Your shirt is not buttoned right," I said with a snicker.

"OH!" she said, looking down at the buttons that she missed, as if she had gotten dressed in the dark. She scurried into the bathroom to fix them.

As she passed by the mirror, heading back into the kitchen, she noticed her wild hair. She used her fingers to comb through her hair.

"Old Man Joe said he was looking for me back in July. I said, Oh yeah?" Auntie Madeline said sounding flattered. "I told him, that they done changed the curriculum at the school and had scheduled the training for all of the teachers in July, so this would have been the first summer that I wasn't gonna make it up here, and then, mmmh! My sister died," she said looking sad, as she headed back into the kitchen.

"Is that why I couldn't get you?" I asked. "I tried to call you right after Momma's fall but your voice mail wasn't set up."

"Yeah, chile. They have us take the test down in the country, where there's no reception. You know I don't carry no cellular phone anyways, and I still don't know how to set up that answering machine," Auntie Mabeline said, sounding shameful, for not being there for Momma.

"Well, you are here now Auntie," I said, attempting to make her feel better.

"I second that," Franklin said, placing the last of the ingredients, that we found to make the pies on the counter.

"What's this for?" she asked.

"Anna Mae is on her way over and she's going to need yours and Grace's help, making pies for the repast," Franklin said.

"What you mean we gotta make pies for the repast?" she asked, looking shocked.

"Well, Pastor Fallback came by yesterday, saying that we may not have enough food and that the diaconate board is going to buy some chicken," Franklin said.

"WHAT! Oh, no they not!" Auntie Mabeline exclaimed.

That's one thing about Auntie Mabeline. She didn't take no mess.

"I'm gonna have a heart to heart talk with Pastor Fallback. All them years I've come up here summer after summer and helped my sister slave down at that church in the soup kitchen, taking her little money to feed them folks, when she had a family of her own. Oh no! She ain't going out like that! Pastor Fallback better come again," she shouted.

I smiled at Auntie Mabeline. Boy, was I glad she was here!

"So, where's David? What have ya'll done with David? Have you locked him in the closet or something? He's too big to be hiding up under this kitchen table," she said, giggling.

"I don't know," I said, "He left out earlier this morning."

"Well, he will not be playing no disappearing acts while I'm here," Auntie Madeline exclaimed.

Good luck with that, I thought.

"Franklin, is there room for one more in the limousine?"

"Huh?" Franklin said.

"Boy, you heard me. I know the Army taught you to listen up the first time," she said. "Old Man Joe needs a ride. He said none of ya'll even told him that your Momma had passed. He just knew it was more quiet than usual and he felt a little more at peace, since no one was knocking down his door for his little rent. "Well, that's because it's the middle of the month," Franklin said. He even said that Anna Mae had dropped a lot of weight and was riding him around town like she was trying to kidnap him. That girl finally got her license?" Auntie Mabeline asked inquisitively.

I laughed. "That was me, Auntie. I took him on an errand after we came from the hospital after Momma passed. I know he's forgetful and he asks a lot of questions, I just wasn't in the mood to tell him about Momma."

"Chile, I can understand that. Now it's coming clear. He said that your hair was sticking up all over the place and Lord knows that Anna Mae is so vain, she ain't gonna let no piece of that short hair she got, get out of place. Gracie, I like the way it looks today," she said, admiring my hair. "But that ain't like you. You use to be in the mirror all the time primping. You'd come out with your hair braided in two neat cornrows going back. I hope you ain't depressed because of what happened to your Momma? Are you?" I remained silent.

CHAPTER 24

Bang! Bang! Bang!

"OPEN THE DOOR!" Anna Mae shouted.

Me and Auntie Mabeline had fallen asleep on the couch, as Tyler Perry's "Diary of A Mad Black Woman," watched us. We had seen it a million times. It was our favorite movie. I could hear Franklin snoring, as he lay asleep across Momma's bed.

"That girl making all that noise like that?" Auntie Mabeline said as if it were a surprise.

I opened the door.

"Grace, help me with these bags," Anna Mae said, rudely.

"There's my favorite Auntie," she said handing me the bags as she bent down to hug Auntie Mabeline, who was laying on the couch, wrapped in Momma's favorite blanket.

"Girl, you sure do know how to keep up a lot of racket," Auntie Mabeline said. "Where is that husband of yours?"

"He just helped me bring all the bags upstairs. I told him that you were flying in today and you want to meet him," Anna Mae said.

While they greeted each other, I had already put the bags on the counter and hurried back into the living room. I sat on the recliner, as I watched Anna Mae, who looked uncomfortable.

"Anna Mae, you jumped up here as soon as you started smelling yourself at eighteen in your hot pants, leaving your Momma when she needed you the most, to chase this no-good fool and it seems like, he's been running from you ever since," Auntie Mabeline said, not mincing her words.

"I'll be right back. I have to put this milk in the refrigerator before it spoils," Anna Mae interrupted; both Aunt Mabeline and the truth she told.

Anna Mae stayed in the kitchen pretending as if she was busy. I followed Auntie Mabeline into the kitchen as she pulled out the kitchen chair and watched Anna Mae put the groceries up.

"Anna Mae!" Auntie Mabeline screeched. "So why didn't Rufus come in to speak? He was not even five feet away from me?"

Anna Mae looked nervous as she placed the milk, into the cabinet. Then realizing her mistake, she grabbed it and marched over to the refrigerator, opening the door and placing the milk on the shelf, purposely not making eye contact with Auntie Mabeline.

"He said that he had to go run some errands and that he may come back. If not, he'll meet you in a few days at the funeral." Anna Mae responded, co-signing Rufus's lies.

"Chile, you have got to get unstuck on sheer stupidity," Auntie Mabeline said.

I sat across from Auntie Mabeline, not saying a word. But I watched her every move eating my imaginary popcorn.

"Your Momma had told me how that so called husband of yours, made snide comments to your own sister, sitting right here. Like he wanted you and her both. You acting like you in denial. I would have checked his behind so quick, that his head would spin," Auntie Mabeline continued, "…you have seen your Momma, firsthand, raise four kids after your Daddy died, with no man in sight. You don't have a child or a chick and you letting this no-good man just put you through the wringer," Auntie Mabeline preached. Like a preacher, she paused to reach for a bottled water sitting on the table; opening it to take a swallow, as she continued her unwelcomed sermon on relationships. "You know, your Momma always thought, that's why you treated this chile here, the way you did," pointing to me, "…because you have so much resentment toward her cause she's free and you living in bondage."

I must've said, "AMEN," in my head a thousand times as I sat there, waving my imaginary lace handkerchief and shouting in my mind, just like I'd seen the people at church do, "Won't He do it! Won't He do it!" I even felt a little kick from my baby inside my belly. God surely sent a ram in the bush in the form of Auntie Mabeline to serve Anna Mae up on a platter. Her sermon came from the book of, good ole' common sense. Preach! I could tell that Anna Mae was listening to Auntie Mabeline. Anna Mae looked as if she wanted to cry but held it back continuing to put the groceries up, not saying a word.

Just when I thought that Auntie Mabeline was done. She took another gulp of her water, sat it on the table with the cap twisted back and said, "Anna Mae, I would stop taking rides,"

I looked at Auntie Mabeline, looking lost by her comment.

"I'm not taking no rides. Rufus takes me where ever I need to go!" she exclaimed. It was a helpless attempt at trying to clap back at Auntie Mabeline.

"Hear me now chile. I'm trying to save you, now that your Momma is gone. Ever since you moved out from this place, your Momma would cry on the phone, about how you were mistreating her. Anything she asked of you, you would tell her that she needed to ask your husband, if you could do "this or that" Auntie Mabeline," mimicking Anna Mae's theatrics. "Your Momma felt like you turned your back on her, putting a man over the very woman who sacrificed for you and your siblings. Hear me now, chile," Auntie Mabeline said. "You taking rides."

Anna Mae stood there shaking her head in disagreement. "No, I'm not!" Anna Mae exclaimed, with an attitude.

"That's the problem chile. He controlling you. He riding you during the day, so you can ride him at night. If you don't wake up from this fantasy of yours, he gonna ride you to the next bus stop and drop you off! Now that's all I've got to say," Auntie Mabeline said. Then she turned to me and said, "Gracie, go on in there and get my pocketbook, so I can take my medicine. This child done raised up my blood pressure!"

CHAPTER 25

In spite of Auntie Mabeline reading Anna Mae, they were both able to work together and bake twelve pies for Momma's repast. Three each of Momma's favorites; pecan, apple, old-fashioned peach and sweet potato. Me and Franklin sat in the kitchen and helped out whenever Anna Mae barked commands at us.

After we shared with Auntie Mabeline what the diaconate board had planned for Momma's repast, Auntie Mabeline got on the phone with Pastor Fallback and let him have it. He called back two hours later with a menu that would even get Momma's stamp of approval. It was 9:30 pm, by the time me and Franklin cleaned the kitchen up and David came walking through the door. He came straight into the kitchen where me, Franklin, Anna Mae and Auntie Mabeline had spent most of the evening, laughing and reminiscing about the past.

"Hey, Auntie Mabeline! How you doing?" He said as he ran over giving Auntie Mabeline a bear hug.

"Boy where you been? I've been waiting to see you since I got here," she said pushing back from his hug, with her hands on her hip. "You smelling like you done fell in some Moonshine, Chile! Where you been?" Auntie Mabeline asked.

We all watched David for his response, to see if he was going to be as flip-mouthed as we'd known him to be.

"Oh, I've been out kicking it with one of my friends," David replied ever so casually.

"You better not have any alcohol up in Momma's house, I know that!" Anna Mae said, going right in on David.

"Anna Mae, save it!" David said and proceeded to take off his dark brown, north face, goose vest and helping himself to the lemon meringue pie that was in the refrigerator.

"Well, don't you start acting a fool now that your Momma is gone. You know, you ain't too old for me to tackle your big behind," Auntie Mabeline said looking David up and down. They both looked at each other and chuckled. "I like that jacket? Is that new? Looks like something I can fit," she said.

David seemed happier today, than I'd seen him since Momma's fall four months earlier. "Auntie Mabeline, it's a vest and what would you look like wearing a man's vest?" he said laughing.

"I don't know. Let me see," she said, joking.

Me, Franklin and Anna Mae just looked at David, as if to say, who are you and what have you done with our brother? Clearly, Aunt Mabeline knew how to reach him.

I was surprised that Franklin didn't say anything. He just looked at David, as if he was trying to read what was going on with him. I'm sure Franklin was wondering, as I had if David was hiding a drinking problem from all of us.

"Oh, did ya'll hear what happened to Big Tuna?" David said leaning up against the door frame, stuffing, half of the slice of pie into his mouth.

"No, what?" Franklin asked. "When we were coming in earlier, we saw him in the backseat of the police car."

"So they did find him," David commented, as he removed his brown leather rhino cap from his head, showing off his fresh new hair cut.

"David, I was wondering how long it was going to take you, to show some respect in your Momma's house. Just because she's gone, don't lose your mind now," Auntie Mabeline said. "I'll have to get that frying pan over there and beat the ever-loving crap out of ya. You know I will," Auntie Mabeline said, referring to David removing his hat in the house and sounding as if she's been a fly on the wall to what had been going on.

"No doubt, Auntie," David remarked. "When did you get so violent?"

David laughed, leaving the rest of us, speechless as he continued on with his story. "Ummm…...where did I leave off?" he said, trying to remember. "So, yeah, I was at the barbershop and the guys were saying that he was on the run. I guess, the same girl that he had abused before, you know, the one that sent him to prison, they found her locked in the trunk of her own car."

"I told you these men are crazy!" Auntie Mabeline said looking directly at Anna Mae.

"Auntie Mabeline, it's probably not a good idea for you to be hanging down at Old Man Joe's," Franklin said.

"Boy, I ain't got nothing that young whipper snapper wants. Besides, he come at me, I got something for him," she said, digging in her bra and pulling out a small bottle of mace.

David's story about Big Tuna scared the living daylights out of me.

"Is she okay?" I asked, "The girl in the trunk. Did she die?"

"No. She ain't dead," David said. "She kicked out the back light at the same time, that some kids were walking by from school. She scared the crap out of them, when they heard her scream and then noticed her bloody foot. That's when they ran to get help."

I got up and ran out the room.

"Oh, my God!" I heard Anna Mae say.

They were all caught up in David's story about Big Tuna, that they didn't realize that I had left.

I went into my room and closed the door. As I leaned up against it, I wondered if Big Tuna was the father of my baby. I remembered the day when me and Old Man Joe got back to the house, from running errands and I noticed that he was wearing timberlands, just like the person who sexually assaulted me. Big Tuna was about the size of the man that I tried to fight off. Should I go tell them what happened? With Auntie Mabeline here, she would make sure that he didn't see the light of day, that's if Franklin didn't get to him first. I wondered, should I tell them all of this, knowing that Momma's funeral is in a few days. But I cannot keep holding this in. Sooner or later, my body will reveal my secret! It's killing me inside knowing that he could be getting away with what he did to me.

CHAPTER 26

I opened my bedroom door and walked back down the hall, into the kitchen, to all of them laughing hysterically. Auntie Mabeline was reminiscing, sharing stories about all of us, from her past summer visits.

"Lord, chile, David," she said, "I remember when you were about three years old. I had come up to help your Momma tend to Gracie, who was about one but wasn't walking yet. The other two were at school," she said pointing in the direction of Franklin and Anna Mae. "Your Momma told me that she was going to the market, but that you were potty trained. I said, alright, that works for me. She knew I couldn't deal with having to change pampers for two of ya'll." Auntie Mabeline leaned back in her chair and continued the story.

"David, you were squirming down the hall there," as she pointed in the direction of the hallway. "You had your legs crossed and squeezed together. I looked at you and said, boy go on in the bathroom and sit on the potty chair. Next thing I know, you screamed at the top of your lungs. I put Gracie down on the sofa and plopped some pillows beside her, so she didn't roll her little self-right off the couch, and ran into the bathroom." Auntie Mabeline started cracking up, laughing. Then looked at us and said, "this boy had his wee wee stuck in his zipper." We all laughed except David, who grimaced, as if he could still feel the pain.

"I remember that day Auntie," David said, shaking his head in disbelief.

"I know that thing must be as long as a snake now, as big as you are!" Auntie Mabeline said. We all laughed.

"Lord, David, I used to feel so bad for you. Especially when this chile here," pointing to Anna Mae, "would not let you eat unless you cleaned up to her liking."

"Yup, Auntie. Now that I'm as big as she is, she can't boss me around no more," he said, with his arms folded while giving Anna Mae the side eye.

"…Or starve your big butt, like she did that time, when me and your Momma had gone out to the curtain factory and left ya'll kids here. When we came back, we heard a noise coming from the pantry. I said, Leola, I think you got some mice in that pantry eating up your food. Well, she grabbed the broom and asked me to open the door, so she can whack the mice in the head. When I ever opened the door and she lifted that broom up, swinging with all her might, but stopped right before she busted David's head wide open," Aunt Mabeline said as she tried to catch her breath from laughing so hard. "Chile, this boy here was in the closet eating T-bones dog biscuits, after Anna Mae wouldn't let him eat because he didn't clean his room," she shared in laughter.

David looked at Anna Mae shaking his head. Anna Mae had a big smirk on her face and said, "Yup! You got to work, to eat!"

"David, do you remember what you said to me and your Momma?" Auntie Mabeline asked.

David laughed and said, "Dog biscuits ain't killed nobody," we all busted out laughing.

"Yup and then T-Bone ran away. Probably because he got sick of competing for his food with you," Franklin said, looking to David.

"Anna Mae, chile, I remember the day that you got your Momma hot as fire. You were about twelve or thirteen. I had just landed back in Georgia, from leaving here, when your Momma called me crying on the phone. I couldn't make out one word she was saying, until after she calmed down," Auntie Mabeline said.

"Your Momma told me that you went to school and told your teacher that your Momma forced you to cook and clean and treated you like Celie from the Color Purple. I recall that day as if it were yesterday. Your Momma said that Child Protective Services came banging on her door," Auntie Mabeline looked at Anna Mae and pointed to the doorway. "She saw you peek around this kitchen doorway, with a dish rag tossed over your shoulder, a handkerchief tied to the front of your head, wearing your little red and white plaid apron, pretending to act just as shocked as your Momma was when they came in the house with their black notebook. It took everything, including the blood of Jesus to keep your Momma from wringing your neck, chile," she said as she unscrewed the bottle of water, taking a dainty sip. "Your Momma told me that, the CPS lady handed her some pamphlets on child abuse and neglect, and added her to a one-year watch list. I had to convince your Momma not to pack your bags and send you my way!"

"I remember that," I said, looking at Anna Mae. After that, it took Momma a good month before she asked Anna Mae for help in the kitchen again.

David looked at Anna Mae and busted out with, the song from the Color Purple movie, "Me and you, us never part," as he pretended to play patty cake with the stove. We all busted out laughing, including Anna Mae.

Auntie Mabeline looked at Franklin and Anna Mae and said, "Boy you weren't always as mature as you are now. You and Anna Mae gave your Momma double the trouble at times," she said.

We hung onto every word that Auntie Mabeline said. She was always a good story teller and never veered from the truth.

"When ya'll were teenagers," she said shaking her head. "I remember the day Franklin came flying in the house from baseball practice. Me and your Momma thought one of them clown men that we heard about on the news, tried to get to you because you came running in this house so fast, like you were sliding into one of them bases out there on the baseball field. It was the first time that your Momma allowed Anna Mae to go with you to baseball practice.

Well, Anna Mae had come home earlier and locked herself up in her room. Me and your Momma were sitting in the kitchen, drinking a cup of coffee and enjoying one of her homemade pecan pies, when Franklin, you came in confessing like you were in one of them catholic booths and we were the priest. You told us that, some of the boys from school were double daring each other to kiss a girl who they were calling "juicy jugs" in the baseball dugout. When it was your turn, you went into the baseball dugout, stunned to find your own sister, with her eyes closed and her full shimmering lips, glossed and puckered up. After that, your Momma kept a short leash on ya'll girls or at least she tried too!" she said, patting me on the hand.

Auntie Mabeline looked at Anna Mae and said, "That's when me and your Momma carried you to the doctor and put your fourteen-year-old butt on them birth control pills." As if she was wearing glasses, Auntie Mabeline tilted her head down, as she looked at Anna Mae and said, "I hope you still taking them!" Making reference to her earlier conversation about Rufus.

"That was crazy" Franklin remarked. He still looked embarrassed about the dugout story, as we laughed.

"I remember that," Anna Mae said, sounding proud of that moment.

"The only one who didn't give your Momma a world of trouble was you, Gracie," Auntie Mabeline said looking right at me. "I think by the time you got to be a teenager, you and your Momma's roles reversed. Once she got sick, you became like her Momma and she became dependent on you." Auntie Mabeline reached for my hand across the table and looked directly in my eyes, "God is gonna always take care of you for being there for your Momma, Gracie, you hear?"

"Yes," I said sadly; wishing Momma could hear her words too.

Auntie Mabeline noticing the sadness in my eyes attempted to lift my spirits she said, "You know that the good Lord has been protecting you. Ever since you could walk, He saved you from these kids attempt to try to take you out," Auntie Mabeline laughed.

"Your older sister over there had you dangling off the porch, thinking that someone was trying to break in. Had she looked through the peep hole, she would have seen that Old Man Joe, got confused and climbed the stairs, thinking he was opening his own door. Your Momma said, she'd pulled up just in the nick of time, as Anna Mae had you dangling like a worm on a hook, over the porch."

Anna Mae, laughed in a sinister kind of way as if she was sorry her attempt failed.

"…Or the time that me and your Momma were hanging our clothes, on the clothes line. We hadn't left ya'll kids for not even fifteen minutes. We came back in, to find that Franklin, Anna Mae, and David had made a homemade rollercoaster, out of your Momma's dining room chairs and a twin mattress. Then they put you in a cardboard box, like you were on a roller coaster. Your Momma came through that door, just in the nick of time to save your forehead from hitting the door stopper," Auntie Mabeline said, shaking her head. "Your hands were straight up in the air" like this, she said, raising both of her hands over her head.

"It was their idea," David said, pointing to Franklin and Anna Mae. We all chuckled.

"You can laugh now," Auntie Mabeline said, "Lord chile, your Momma gave you the right name. Because if it wasn't for God's amazing grace, them kids would have killed you a long time ago."

David walked over to Auntie Mabeline, putting his hands on her shoulders as if he was giving her a massage.

"Auntie, since you want to walk down memory lane at our expense," David said in a teasing kind of way, "Do you remember the day you walked to the corner store up there?" He said, pointing into the direction of Petra's Market. "… when Momma asked you to pick up some toilet paper?" He could barely finish his sentence before we all laughed, remembering the lesson that Auntie Mabeline tried to teach us that day, even though it didn't stick.

"That was funny," I said. I smiled just thinking about it waiting for David to finish telling the story.

"You came back here steaming because you had to spend five dollars on some toilet paper. Momma tried to explain to you, that there's five of us and one of you, so of course, you were going to be sticker shocked. But you weren't hearing it," he said and the room roared in laughter.

"You had Grace round us all up. I think she was probably about seven and you said, "pick a seat." Any old one will do," like we were your students in your classroom. You busted open the package of toilet paper and took one roll out. You said, "There is no excuse for ya'll to be going through toilet paper like you drank that purple Kool-aid." You held up the toilet paper and said, "See this," as you pulled two sheets at the perforated line, you said, "This is the most toilet paper that you need, to wipe that nasty butt of yours. And this roll better last until I leave."" We all fell out laughing.

"Yup!" Franklin said, "then Momma sent me and David to the store to buy more, so you would think that it lasted for two months."

"You little sneaky scoundrels," Auntie Mabeline said as she continued to laugh hysterically.

Anna Mae laughed so hard, that she spilled water on her jumpsuit.

"Auntie, show me what you are wearing to the funeral," she blurted out, dabbing the water that did not trickle down her cleavage.

"Well, I am not staying for this," David said.

"I'm right behind you," Franklin said and the two of them headed to the living room to watch television.

As David passed by me, he yanked on the back of my straight, flat ironed hair.

"Cut it out, nutty professor!" I yelled.

"David, if you don't leave your sister alone! You used to be stuck to this child like glue. Sleeping right up in the bed next to her. Your Momma couldn't keep you out of her room, especially when you would eat up them chocolate cakes that she would bake for you in her Easy Bake Oven," Aunt Mabeline said and laughed some more.

"Now he eating whole cakes and pies!" Anna Mae said, taking a jab at David.

CHAPTER 27

Auntie Mabeline turned around in the kitchen in the dress that she planned to wear to Momma's funeral. I laughed, as I looked at Anna Mae's expression, as she stood there in her Army green Michael Kors jumpsuit, with her gold Guess t-strap sandals looking, up and down at Auntie Mabeline, in disapproval.

"OH NO!" She said, covering her hand with her mouth.

Auntie Mabeline looked stunning! She looked as if she was going to a formal party but not her sister's funeral.

"Auntie Mabeline, you don't get out much, huh?" Anna Mae said.

Auntie Mabeline looked down as if she couldn't see what was wrong with her outfit. She had on a long, tightly fitted black sequins dress with a little train in the back; her gut looking just as big as her butt.

"Is that all you brought?" I asked.

"Chile yeah," she cut her eyes at me as if I shouldn't be questioning her.

"Never mind my attire?" she said, looking at me, "What are you wearing?"

I pulled myself into the table as if to hide my stomach. "I'm wearing my black dress and my black patent leather wedges," I said. I didn't dare mention the ruching that would cover my stomach.

I shifted the focus off of me and back onto Auntie Mabeline.

"Well, Momma was the same size as you, so I'm sure she got something in her closet that you can fit," I said.

As soon as I said that, Anna Mae high tailed it, straight to Momma's closet. It didn't take her long to find a black suit, that Momma hadn't worn yet; that still had the tags on it and a matching hat, saving me from having to take Auntie Mabeline shopping.

"This will work and it gives you the sprinkle of flashiness that you are looking for," Anna Mae said. Spoken like a true self-made fashion expert. She handed the two-piece suit with sequins around the collar, wrist, and pockets, to Auntie Mabeline.

"Chile, this is probably the outfit that your Momma wanted to be buried in," Auntie Mabeline said, holding it up.

"No, Auntie Mabeline," I said. "Momma told me and Anna Mae what she wanted to wear a long time ago. Momma said, she didn't want to be dressed all in black as if she was attending her own funeral. Her favorite color was peach," I said.

Auntie Mabeline said, as if I thought that she didn't know her own sister, "Chile, I know that."

As if she was trying to build Rufus's reputation, Anna Mae blurted out, "Rufus took me to the funeral home, before I came here, to drop off Momma's outfit that she wanted to be buried in. Momma had been asked Misty to do her hair. I called her this morning and told her that Momma had passed and reminded her of Momma's wishes," Anna Mae said. Not having a clue that Misty already knew about Momma's passing, when I told her the other day. "She said, it would be an honor to do Momma's hair," Anna Mae said.

"What else did Misty say?" I asked.

"Nothing. Why?" Anna Mae asked.

"You're telling us stuff that we already know," I said.

It wasn't hard to get Anna Mae to lose her train of thought.

"Shut up Grace!" Anna Mae exclaimed. "Now, what was I saying?"

"Chile, first off, stop telling your sister to shut up. Second, if you can't remember, as I tell my students, then it wasn't that damn important" Auntie Mabeline said, still standing there admiring the suit, that she'd hung over the cabinet door.

I covered my mouth and giggled under my breath. As if she was reminding Anna Mae what she had been talking about, Auntie Mabeline said, "Yeah, your Momma was quite fond of that chile, Misty. I like her too. Your Momma appreciated that she did her hair for free," she said. "That's a nice, wholesome girl right there. I don't know why David or Franklin hadn't picked up on that."

"Misty don't want neither one of them," Anna Mae said. "She always said that Franklin and David are like brothers to her."

"Especially not David. He's too lazy," I said.

"Speaking of Misty," Anna Mae said as if we had gotten off subject.

My heart sank to my stomach. Was Anna Mae about to say it? Was she about to reveal what I shared with Misty?

"Me and Grace have a hair appointment on Friday. Did you want me to make you one too?" she asked Auntie Mabeline.

Auntie Mabeline sat the big black Minx hat on the table, still standing in her sequins dress. She said, "Chile no! Them girls in that salon, keep them people way too long, running everybody's business but their own. Ain't nobody got time for that! People got things to do, people to meet and places to be. I don't need to throw my little bit of money away. I like Misty, but she ain't gonna do my hair for free, especially knowing that I got a good job as a teacher," she said. "Ya'll rich girls, go ahead on down there. I can do my hair just fine!" she said.

Auntie Mabeline removed Momma's black two-piece suit from over the cabinet.

"Gracie, unzip this thing for me," she beckoned to me before she walked out of the kitchen.

I unzipped Auntie Mabeline's sequin dress. She reappeared ten minutes later, wearing Momma's black sequins suit and looking more appropriately dressed for Momma's funeral.

"Try it with the hat on," Anna Mae said, fixing it on top of Auntie Mabeline's head.

"Auntie, you look really nice," I said.

"Now, that's much better, you know what I'm sayin'?" Anna Mae said. She then looked up to the ceiling, "You're welcome, Momma!" we all laughed.

Chapter 28

The week had flown by since Auntie Mabeline arrived on Wednesday. It was Friday, the day of my and Anna Mae's hair appointment and the day before Momma's funeral. I didn't know which one I dreaded most. Going to the salon, after Anna Mae foolishly failed to disconnect the three-way call or coming to terms that Momma is never coming back.

"Gracie," Auntie Mabeline yelled in a soulful singing way.

I walked into the kitchen, to see that she'd made some scrambled eggs, grits, bacon and homemade biscuits.

Auntie Mabeline was a good cook, just like Momma and Anna Mae. I know Momma would have taught me too, had she not gotten sick.

"Good morning, Auntie," I said. I gave her a side hug while she wiped down the stove.

"Good morning, Gracie. Did you sleep well?" she asked.

"I did," I said and paused watching her clean just like Momma. "Oh. I'm sorry Auntie. I forgot to ask you, how did you sleep? Momma had been meaning to buy a new mattress. We could switch rooms, if Momma's bed is too uncomfortable," I said.

"Oh, chile. I'm from the south. We make do with what we have. I threw some of them comforters that she had folded up in her closet on the bed. So, I was good," Auntie Mabeline said.

"Both of your brothers got up and went out to Burlington Coat Factory to look for them a black suit," she said. "I don't know why they waited to the last minute, knowing that your Momma's funeral is tomorrow?"

"Oh," I said. Now understanding why the house was so peaceful.

"You know I had to stay in this kitchen and make sure they didn't eat up all of the food from you," we both laughed.

"Thank you, Auntie! Appreciate ya," I giggled mocking her.

Auntie Mabeline took the dish rag from her shoulder and slapped me on the behind with it, in a playful way, as we laughed.

"So, what are ya'll going to do with all them clothes your Momma got in her closet?" she asked.

"We decided to donate them. Anna Mae wants us to go through them and pack them up for good will," I said. "Auntie, you can take what you want. I know Anna Mae won't mind. Besides, if Momma was going to give her clothes to anyone, you know she would want you to have them," I said.

"Yeah, you right, Chile but remember, I only came with one suitcase and that's packed to capacity already. Plus, I'm gonna get David or Franklin one to run me over to Roxie's supermarket before I leave out on Sunday, so I can pick me up some of them fine spareribs they got over there and bring them back to Georgia," she said.

No one knew, besides me that David had lost his license.

"Auntie, I can take you over there on Sunday," I said.

"Chile, you so petite, I keep forgetting that you have your license, looking like that Toni Braxton, chile," she said. "You just cute as a button. Even with that extra weight you done gained in your face. Now that your Momma is gone, don't you take up after your brother and start eating everything in sight. That butt of yours is big enough," she laughed.

"But seriously Gracie, learn that lesson from your Momma. When you're on a fixed income, you have to learn how to make things last."

"Okay, Auntie," I said in agreement and with a half-smile. "You do know I have a job, right?"

"Even with a job, you have to learn to live within your means," she said. "Learn to save your money. One day you gonna want to retire like I'll be doing pretty soon. You want to make sure you got a good little nest egg to sit on. You hear me, chile?" Aunt Mabeline asked.

"Yeah, I do," I said.

"You make sure you know the difference between a want and a need," she said looking at her watch. "Speaking of a "want," don't you and Anna Mae have a hair appointment today?" she asked.

"Yes, we do," I said, sounding unexcited.

"Well, fix you a plate and eat so you can be ready to go when she comes. Lord knows, if I have to hear that girl say, "you know what I'm sayin," one more time, I'm gonna jump off of that porch out there," we both laughed.

CHAPTER 29

As we walked into the hair salon, I was so embarrassed by the voice message that we'd left last week, on the answering machine. If it wasn't for Momma's funeral, I would have played a "no show."

"Hey Anna Mae. Hey there Grace," Misty said, putting down the can of hair spray, as she walked over to greet us.

"I'm so sorry for the loss of Ms. Leola," she whispered to each of us as if she hadn't told us before. "I plan to go down to the funeral home, early in the morning to do her hair, before they dress her body."

"Thank you," I said.

Anna Mae didn't hear anything that Misty had said because she was too busy, leaning on the counter adjacent to Kia, the receptionist desk, making sexually suggested advances with her eyes toward the not so attractive, toothless guy, who sat in the barber's chair. She danced with his eyes, right toward her cleavage, that looked like two big cantaloupes. I'd never seen Anna Mae flirt like this before; not with a man other than Rufus. Maybe she misunderstood what Auntie Mabeline was trying to tell her the other day. I went and sat down, thinking that Anna Mae was going to check us both in.

Anna Mae didn't see Misty walk towards me.

"I know you miss your Momma but are you feeling okay?" Misty said using subliminal messages to ask me how was I feeling.

"I'm good," I said, in a low tone.

I always admired her style.

I watched her, as she walked assuredly back over to her client who was sitting in the chair. She picked up the hair spray, liberally spraying it over the clients perfectly done hairdo. Her leopard off the shoulder, form-fitted jumper, complimented her skin tone and chunky jewelry. I used to look forward to coming to the hair shop back in the day with Momma and Anna Mae. I would sit far in the corner, out of Momma's sight, as I looked at all the sexy men in the Jet Magazines. That was back when Momma only let me get my hair done on special occasions or holidays, which meant school picture time and Easter. I would listen to the hairdressers gossip about everything and everybody under the sun, except for Misty who remained above the fray. I would leave out, knowing more things about life, than I did before I walked in.

Once I started making my own money, I would come by myself, after Anna Mae moved out with Rufus. I stopped coming once Momma got too sick for me to leave her home alone. Misty was different than the other two hair stylists, Vonda and Dalia, who seemed to be catty, anytime Misty wasn't around. She never had a bad thing to say about anybody. She was so attentive and caring to her clients. She would ask them how they were doing or inquire about an exciting event that they had last shared with her. She was real, as real could be.

Kia sat at the front desk filing her hot pink nails, popping her gum, as she waiting for Anna Mae to get out of her trance with the ugly guy, who sat in the barber's chair.

"Hey Vonda," Anna Mae said oddly waving and looking back at me as if to snitch on me.

Vonda looked at Anna Mae with a puzzled look and said, "Hey girl," as she side stepped over to Dalia, holding her blow-dryer facing toward the ground asking, "Dalia, is she my client? I don't know her."

Dalia shrugged her shoulders, not seeming to be a part of Anna Mae's fan club either.

"Can I help you?" Kia asked.

"I have an eleven o'clock appointment with Misty," Anna Mae said, sounding all important.

Kia stopped filing her nails, as she scrolled through the appointment book and asked, "and your name is?"

Anna Mae jerked her neck from left to right, "Girl, stop playing. You know who I am."

Kia took her eyes off of the appointment book and looked up at Anna Mae, purposely speaking Ebonics, and said, "No I don't know who you is. Your name is?"

Anna Mae sucked her teeth, saying, "I'm Anna Mae and my sister can speak for herself," pointing at me, as if she remembered that I had a voice.

I reluctantly approached Kia, sitting at the desk, hoping that whoever listened to the voice message, did not recognize my voice.

In a soft-spoken voice, I said, "I'm Grace. I have an 11:30 appointment with Vonda."

"I'm sorry honey. I can't hear you. Can you speak up?" Kia asked.

I wanted, so bad to roll my eyes, but I could hear Momma's voice, plain as day in my head. I cleared my throat and repeated what I'd said to Kia.

She scrolled through the book until she came to the page that said, "Vonda's appointment schedule," placing a check mark next to my name. "Okay, Grace. You're all set."

As I reached for a Mary Jane from the bowl on her desk that had a sticky note that said, "just take one," Kia, in an instant realized that it was me and Anna Mae who had left the voice message the other day. She stood up, leaning over her desk, with her face a foot away from mine.

"Don't worry Grace, I deleted the message that you and your sister left. I didn't mention your name but I asked Misty to address your concern. Besides, you are not the only person who's complained about that," she whispered. She reached into her desk drawer and handed me a hair book titled, "Natural Hair Styles for Black Women." You may find a style in here that you like," she said with a warm smile.

I smiled back, relieved that Kia looked out for me, unlike Anna Mae.

I walked to the waiting area, where Anna Mae was, with a little more pep in my step.

I sat down next to Anna Mae, who was engrossed in the Jet Magazine article, "In Love, A 'Good Guy' Doesn't Exist."

CHAPTER 30

Misty had finally finished Anna Mae's hair and had three clients waiting for her. One client was burning up like the smell of singed hair. She was so mad that she complained to the receptionist twice about Anna Mae and the fact that she had been waiting for over one hour. The woman had a right to be annoyed. Every last one of us had enough of Anna Mae. We listened, for the past hour to her change her mind, as to how she wanted the "four inches" of her hair styled. I could tell that Misty had enough when I overheard her tell Anna Mae, as I was getting my hair washed, "Girl, I'm a beautician, not a magician. You don't have enough hair for that style and I don't have time to do a weave but I can sell you a wig."

"Okay, girl, well hook me up," Anna Mae said, finally shutting up.

Anna Mae stood in front of me, primping in the mirror, as I lifted the hair dryer from my head, ready for Vonda to rinse the deep conditioner out and blow-dry my hair.

"Misty, girl, you got my hair laid!" Anna Mae said.

Misty had done Anna Mae's hair, just like she had done it every other time before, tight curls all over, with the front hanging down forming a curly bang.

Anna Mae walked over to me.

"Grace, I'm going next door to get me a drink," so consumed with herself, she didn't even ask me if I wanted anything, which I didn't.

Anna Mae stopped at Kia's desk and paid her bill and then headed for the door. "She's on her own," she said, pointing to me.

"Anna Mae, are you going next door to the store?" Misty asked.

"Yes, girl. I've been sitting in that chair for over an hour. I need a snack," Anna Mae said, as if it was Misty's fault.

"I'll go with you," Misty said, grabbing her change purse from her station and ignoring Anna Mae's comment.

Misty looked over at the woman who had been waiting over an hour. "Just give me five minutes."

The woman stood up, shook her head, looked at her watch and sat back down. Misty was well known around the city, as being one of the best beauticians south of Boston. She was well worth the wait.

"Does anyone want anything?" Misty yelled. Everyone said no. Misty looked at me, "Grace, can I get you something?" I was still full from the large breakfast that Auntie Mabeline cooked. "No thank you. But thanks for asking, Misty," I said.

Misty smiled, as she and Anna Mae walked out of the door. Vonda and Dalia, the other hairdresser began to chat it up, as if Misty was the cat and they were the mice.

"Did you hear that Ms. Leola passed?" Dalia, who looked to be about my age, asked Vonda.

"Who's that?" Vonda said, "I don't know no Ms. Leola."

They both chuckled.

It was obvious that Dalia hadn't recognized me, from when I used to come in and get my hair done. Probably because I was so quiet and I sat in the corner getting up, just to get my hair done and leave.

"Girl, everybody who's anybody, knew who Ms. Leola was. Misty used to do her hair for free. She would bring in her homemade pecan pies and banana pudding here into the shop. They would be gone, faster than moving cockroaches. She ran the soup kitchen down at the church. She fed everybody, whether you were homeless or not. People would be lined up for seconds. There was no shame, in their game. She put her foot in her food," Dalia said as if she remembered that Vonda hadn't worked at the shop, as long as she had. She continued and said, "Oh girl, I forgot, she used to come in before you started working here, so you probably don't remember her. She was really nice but she was strict," she recalled.

"My sister used to volunteer back in the day when she was a teenager down at the soup kitchen with some of the other kids from church. Ms. Leola's kids would be right there too. My sister used to come home complaining about that one bossy daughter of hers; that wore them bifocals. But as for Ms. Leola, she and my sister had gotten so close, that she would send my sister home with leftover soup and pies. Girl, we would tear that food up! My sister said that Ms. Leola didn't play but she treated all of them kids as if they were her own," she continued.

"My sister was all messed up the other night when she heard that Ms. Leola had passed. I guess she'd stopped running the soup kitchen a few years ago. She had gotten so sick and could barely walk but she was well respected here in the community."

Dalia, removed the hot comb from its chamber, as she used it as a pointer, saying, "She lived over there."

Vonda, not even looking up from flat ironing my hair, said, "Oh yeah, I don't know her."

I sat there, silent as a church mouse, as I watched the hairdresser point into the direction of Momma's house.

"I'm going with my sister to the funeral, just so I can see that fine son of hers. She has two sons. But the older one, who's my sister's age, girl, I would drink his bath water," Dalia laughed. "My sister told me, that he had gone off into the service right after they finished high school. She tried to find him on Facebook and Instagram, but it looked like he doesn't do social media. I guess he ain't about that life," Dalia said, putting the hot comb back into the chamber.

Dalia, ran her hands up and down the sides of her shapely body, as she palmed her breasts, saying, "Now that I'm older and I've filled out in all the right places, I'm going with my sister and her husband to Ms. Leola's funeral just to see him. I already know what I'm wearing.

I'm going to rock my skin tight, sexy black dress, with my bright red matching bra and thong under it. You already know what times it is."

They both started laughing.

I sat there fuming about Dalia's cold-hearted, calculated plans to seduce Franklin, at our own Momma's funeral. I sat there thinking, had Auntie Mabeline came with us and heard Dalia talk like this, she would have set it off up in this salon.

"Girl, you are a hot mess," Vonda said to Dalia.

"Girl, I'm serious. I need me a hustler like that, so we can build our own empire.

I remember back in the day, after school, he drove around that noisy ice cream truck, through our neighborhood. His little sister used to help him sell ice cream.

Not that I was checking her out, but she was a spitting image of Toni Braxton, with her perfect cantaloupe breast and little round bubble butt.

I'd seen her around school, once or twice but she wasn't popular. Ms. Leola didn't let her go to any of the school functions or parties but my egg head cousin had a serious crush on that girl.

He would come to our house after school. When he heard the clown music coming from the ice cream truck, he would drop whatever he was doing and run out there, knowing he didn't have no money," Dalia said.

I sat in the chair, remembering how I use to get so excited when Franklin would ask me to help him on the ice cream truck. But I sat there wondering what cousin could she be talking about? Then again, I was in no position to worry my head about it, as I rested my folded hands on my growing belly.

"I wonder what ever became of her? My sister said Ms. Leola had her daughters on lock down. Now that she's gone, I know they are gonna wild out," Dalia said.

"Girl, you know that's right. They are going to be getting it in," Vonda said, as they both cracked up laughing.

I sat frozen in the chair, with mixed emotions, not knowing whether I should scream or cry.

Granted, my face had filled out, from the seven pounds that I'd gained, but it was obvious, that I still looked a mirror image of who I once was.

Our attention turned toward the noise from the chimes that hung on the door, as Misty and Anna Mae returned from the convenient store.

Misty was consoling a sobbing Anna Mae, who seemed to have had a breakdown in the short time that they were gone.

"It's going to be okay. I can only imagine how you and Grace feel," Misty said. She hugged Anna Mae, her arms barely reaching around Anna Mae's wide back.

Dalia looked at Anna Mae, with a smirk on her face and said, "Girl, why are you crying? You left here all happy about your hair, talking about it being laid, slayed and dyed to the side," adding more onto what Anna Mae actually said in efforts to try and make her smile.

With one hand on her hip, she looked at Misty and said, "You must've told her that you are about to jack up the prices. Well, hell, I'd cry too," she said as she reached for the smoky hot comb again.

Misty gave the hairdresser a stern look and said, "She and her sister Grace, lost their mother, Ms. Leola," she said looking my way.

Dalia was speechless, as she looked at me, with her mouth wide open, as if she was trying to remember all that she had said about my family.

"OUCH!" I screamed as Vonda singed my ear with the curling iron.

CHAPTER 31

It was the day of Momma's funeral.

Auntie Mabeline found Momma's Mahalia Jackson CD and she had "His Eye Is on the Sparrow," on blast. I dreaded getting out of bed and wanted to pull the covers over my head. It sounded like Momma's funeral was taking place right in our apartment. I could hear Auntie Mabeline sing along with the music. I never knew she had such a beautiful voice.

"Ya'll need to get up now. You know we can't be late to the church. The limousine will be here at 9:30 this morning," Auntie Mabeline yelled from the hallway. Then she continued to sing with Mahalia. I realized that I hadn't prayed in a long time but knew that if I ever needed Jesus, I would need him today; on the day, we lay Momma to rest. I got up out of bed and knelt down on my knees, facing my bed.

"Dear God, please forgive me for being angry at you for taking my Momma away from me. Please give me the strength to keep it together because Momma would want me to be strong. Please bless the baby that is growing inside of my stomach. I know it's not my will God but Momma always said that you will not give us more than we can bear. And God, can you please keep Anna Mae and David from getting on my last nerve today? Thank you." I felt better taking a moment to pray. Then, I got up to get ready.

"Oh!" I said, shrieking from the swift kick from my baby. It was as if he/she was touching and agreeing with my prayer and also reminding me that I had an appointment next week with the obstetrician.

I grabbed my robe from behind the door, as I looked at myself in my full-length mirror before heading to the kitchen.

"Good morning, Auntie," I said as I snuck one of her biscuits that sat on the table, along with hot link sausages, scrambled eggs, grits and salmon cakes.

"Good morning, Gracie," Auntie Mabeline replied. I could tell she had been crying.

"Are you okay, Auntie?" I asked.

Auntie Mabeline sat down in the chair and wept. Mahalia continued to sing in the background. Auntie Mabeline had seemed so different today, than she had been the past few days.

"Chile, I'm going to be alright. I just miss my sister so much. I cannot believe that she is gone," she said solemnly.

Auntie Mabeline had been so strong for us since she arrived. She hadn't broken down since she'd gotten off of the plane, until now.

I handed her some Kleenex.

She wiped her eyes and said, "Thanks, Gracie. I'm going to be alright. Go on in there and wake your brothers up. They both sleep like logs in the forest," she said.

"Okay," I said, as I gave Auntie Mabeline a huge hug.

"Thank you, Gracie. I needed that," she said.

"I cannot wait to see that pretty hair of yours," she said.

I touched my silk pink bonnet, "You'll be surprised," I said smiling.

I walked out of the kitchen and passed by David's bedroom and knocked on the door.

There was no answer, which was not unusual for David but what was equally unusual was not hearing the sound of him snoring.

"David." I called. But there was still no answer.

Apparently, I had woken Franklin up in the process, who was walking toward me wiping his sleepy eyes.

Just as Franklin got near David's door, I opened it up to find David's bed all made up.

"Where's David?" I said looking at Franklin.

"He's not in there?" Franklin said as he walked into David's bedroom.

"Ah, no! I don't see him and he's too big to fit under his bed," I said.

While Franklin inspected David's closet to make sure he wasn't curled up in it somewhere, I went to the bathroom. No David.

"He's not in here," I yelled.

Franklin and I went to the kitchen. "Good morning, Auntie," Franklin said, "Have you seen David?"

"No!" she said, holding onto her heart.

"Well, he is definitely not here," Franklin said. We both started to fix our plate for breakfast.

"Maybe Anna Mae knows where he's at," Auntie Mabeline said.

"Nope," Franklin said. "She sent me a text message and said that she and Rufus will be here at 8:45 am. She didn't mention David."

"Didn't I say I didn't want the boy playing any disappearing acts, while I'm here?" Auntie Mabeline asked. She was getting upset.

"Yes, you did, Auntie," I said, "But you said it to us, not him," I replied sitting down to eat my breakfast.

"Well, it's 7:45 am now," Franklin said, "Let's just hope that he comes in. If he doesn't, we will have to find someone to sing in his place."

"Well, we don't have to look far," I said.

"What are you talking about, Grace?" Franklin said.

"I heard Auntie Mabeline sing this morning and she has a beautiful voice," I said.

Auntie Mabeline, looked nervous. "Now chile, there's a difference in singing in your own kitchen or the bathroom and singing in front of a hundred judges, staring at you, listening to make sure you hitting the right note, like that show I saw you watch the other night," she said.

"American Idol?" I asked.

"Yeah that one," she said.

"You know, some of them church folk can be brutal," she said.

"Auntie, you'll have to do it for Momma, not for them," I said. I tried to be encouraging toward her, like she had encouraged me on yesterday.

"Lord, ya'll stressing me out. You got me perspiring all ready, sweating out my deodorant," Auntie Mabeline said, unzipping her robe and using a paper plate to fan her body.

Auntie Mabeline looked at me, "Gracie, you know what time it is?"

I smirked.

"Yes, Auntie. It's time for you to take your high blood pressure medicine. I'll go get your pocketbook."

CHAPTER 32

It was 8:30 am and David still had not come home. Auntie Mabeline had found Momma's stash of Negro spirituals. She had replaced Mahalia Jackson with Wallace Willis, singing "Swing Low, Sweet Chariot," while we all were getting dressed. I was in my room putting the finishing touches on. My size eight black, short sleeve dress looked adorable. The ruching hid my stomach perfectly, as the bottom, gave me a little flair. I stuck my foot in my patent leather wedges, that I got on sale at DSW. I opened my purple glass jewelry box and took out the matching pearl earrings, necklace, and bracelet, that Momma gave me and put them on, which finished off my look. I stood in the mirror, primping like Anna Mae, admiring the beautiful job that Vonda had did on my hair, even though my ear was still a little sore.

I saw Franklin pass by my bedroom, looking very handsome. He had on the black suit that he and David shopped for on yesterday. He wore the peach carnation, on his lapel; that we all decided to wear since it was Momma's favorite color. I could hear Auntie Mabeline in Momma's bathroom talking to herself. As I approached the bathroom,

I realized she wasn't talking to herself, she was talking to someone on the phone.

"Now you make sure you are good and ready and don't come out the house wearing all that Brut, that you had on the other night," Auntie Mabeline said, grinning, not realizing that I was standing in the doorway, as she looked out of the bathroom window, with her back toward me. "Okay. See you soon," she hung up.

"Gracie, gal come in here and help me before I rip this skirt!" she yelled.

"I'm right here," I said.

"AH!" She screamed. "Chile, you are going to get enough of sneaking up on me."

As I struggled to zip Auntie Mabeline's size 24 skirt, she exclaimed. "Gracie, I love it!" she said pulling down on one of my long spiral curls as it sprung back into place.

"Thank you, Auntie! Outside of Vonda burning my ear, she did do a good job on my hair," I said prancing some more in the mirror.

"Chile, I didn't call you in here for that! Help me zip this skirt," Auntie Mabeline said. I giggled.

"You look really nice, Auntie!" I said. "I think Momma got some earrings to match this outfit."

"Chile, I don't have no holes in my ears," she said.

"Auntie, they are clip-ons," I said. I went to Momma's jewelry box and picked out the white diamond and black crystal earrings.

"Aww, these are nice. Too nice for my beer pocketbook but I'll wear them," she said and clipped the earrings on her ears.

"I'm gonna throw some curls in my hair and then I will be ready," Auntie Mabeline said.

"Okay. I'll go help Franklin pack up the pies," I said.

"Okay, Gracie," she said.

Just as I was walking out of the bathroom, there was a knock at the front door.

"That must be Anna Mae and Rufus," I said aloud.

I heard Franklin yell, "OH MY GOD! WHAT THE HECK HAPPENED TO YOU!"

"Me and Auntie Mabeline hurried into the living room, as David stumbled in, looking as if he had gotten into a fight. He reeked of alcohol."

"Lord, boy you are going to be the death of me on the same day of my sister's funeral," Auntie Mabeline yelled. She took a seat while Franklin and I tended to David.

David's clothes were ripped and his eye was practically closed shut.

"What happened?" Franklin asked.

"I got into a fight with this dude because he stepped on my shoe," David said slurring his words.

I had never seen David look this bad in my whole life.

"Well, the limousine will be here soon and there is no way that you are going to Momma's funeral in this type of condition," Franklin said, making an executive decision for all of us.

"Plus, you stank!" Auntie Mabeline said. "Seeing you like this David would break your Momma's heart."

I had gone into the bathroom to get a wet wash cloth for David and brought it back to him so he could clean his face.

David didn't even notice me handing him the wash cloth, as he stumbled, right by me. He held onto the wall, as he headed toward his bedroom and fell onto his bed.

Auntie Mabeline looked at Franklin and said, "Something is going on with that boy. I don't know what it is but your Momma even said, ever since he had started smelling himself, he had started to change."

" What does that mean, "smelling himself?" I asked.

"Chile, I am on summer break from being anybody's teacher," Auntie Mabeline said. Then she got up and walked back into the bathroom to finish her hair.

Franklin looked at me, looking concerned about David. "That means once he starts to hit puberty and his body changes."

"Oh!" I said.

We could hear Anna Mae and Rufus come up the steps.

"The limousine is downstairs," she said as she came in through the partially opened door. "I told him to give us fifteen minutes."

Anna Mae walked into the living room and down the hall, leading to the kitchen. "What is that awful smell," she asked passing by David's room.

"Hi, to you too," Franklin said.

"Hey Rufus. I almost forgot what you looked like man," Franklin said, as he shook Rufus' hand and gave him a half hug.

"Hi, Grace. No hug?" Rufus said.

"Hi," I said. I wasn't going nowhere near Rufus. I followed Anna Mae into the kitchen.

"Grace, where is Auntie Mabeline," Anna Mae asked. She turned around in her two-piece, Giorgio Armani black suit, with satin on the collar and sleeves. The diamond emblem that adorned her sleeves, matched her necklace, earrings and the jewel on her Manolo Blahnik black pumps.

"I'm right here, Chile," Auntie Mabeline said coming out of the bathroom.

"Look at you!" Anna Mae said. "You looking good, Auntie Mabeline."

Franklin and Rufus met us in the kitchen.

"And who is this?" Auntie Mabeline said looking at Rufus who was dressed in a black shirt and pants with no suit jacket. Much simpler than Anna Mae.

"Auntie Mabeline this is my husband Rufus," Anna Mae said.

"Auntie. I have heard so much about you," Rufus said, as he came over and gave Auntie Mabeline a very affectionate hug, rubbing her back up and down, moving his hand closer to her large bum.

"Boy, I ain't your aunt! You ain't no kin to me!" Auntie Mabeline said, pushing away from Rufus. "And I hope you didn't get any of that jerry curl juice on my suit," she said as she started feeling her shoulders for wet spots. "Didn't that style go out in the 80's?"

Rufus, looking embarrassed, went and stood near the kitchen door, as if he was looking for the great escape, away from Auntie Mabeline.

"And what's that's hanging off your hip?" Auntie Mabeline said as she shook her head in disbelief.

Anna Mae ran over and pulled the $12.99 Walmart tag from the side of Rufus' pants.

Franklin attempted to change the subject before Auntie Mabeline went in on Rufus some more.

"Anna Mae, we have a change in the program," Franklin said.

"What?" she asked.

"David got into some sort of scuffle and is in his room asleep and hungover. So, he's not going to make it. He's pretty messed up," Franklin said.

Anna Mae marched out of the kitchen, her hips almost as wide as the door frame, right into David's room and right back into the kitchen, where we all were. Her hands shot straight up in the air and she was fuming.

"OH, MY GOD! He's supposed to sing Momma's song!" she exclaimed.

"We found a replacement," I said.

"Oh, heck no! Grace, you are not going to embarrass us, with that high pitch Mariah Carey voice of yours!" she said.

"Chile, hush your mouth!" Auntie Mabeline said.

"Auntie Mabeline is going to sing," Franklin said leaning back against the counter, waiting for Anna Mae's reaction.

"Oh no! Auntie Mabeline, you are going to have to sing something now! I don't care if it's one of them nursery rhymes that you sing with them kids in your class, but I need to know that you can carry a tune and that you are not going to put all of us to sleep!" Anna Mae said.

"Chile, who do you think you are talking to? I think you got me mixed up with this fool standing right here," Auntie Mabeline pointed to Rufus.

"Can we all just get along?" Rufus asked.

Auntie Mabeline put her hands on her hip. "Yeah, carry your wife on out of here, how about that!"

"Honk! Honk!"

The limousine driver honked his horn, at the right time, breaking up the tension in the kitchen.

We all hurried out of the kitchen to get downstairs, passing by David's bedroom, as he laid across his bed, knocked out.

"Oh, chile! Ya'll trying to kill me up in here. Got my face makeup all running. Don't forget them pies!" Auntie Mabeline exclaimed.

CHAPTER 33

Momma looked stunning in the shiny peach casket that she picked out months before. She laid there wearing her peach dress with creme color sequins around the neck and waist, close in design to what Auntie Mabeline had on. Her hat was big and beautiful, adorned with fresh pink, peach and white Peonies. Misty had Momma looking casket sharp. Her hair was in a perfectly cut bob hair style, that contoured to her plump little face. Misty had also made up Momma's face, making it look soft, just like Momma's blemish free skin.

I don't know what Auntie Mabeline said to Pastor Fallback but the church was done up to perfection. The front of the church had massive peach, white and pink carnations, that were placed in a half moon, spreading to the back of Momma's casket. There were so many flowers, Momma's body looked like she was lying in state, at the Capitol. The rose heart that I heard Anna Mae order, looked beautiful as it stood on an easel next to Momma's head that spelled out "M-O-M-M-A" in the center.

Auntie Mabeline sat on the edge of the pew, looking for the flower she had asked Anna Mae to order. When she spotted the huge Treasured Lilies Spray, that stood at the foot of Momma's casket, she smiled and whispered, as if she was talking to Momma, "Yeah, I see it. Just beautiful,"

It was getting close to 11:00 am. Momma's service was about start in a few minutes. Me, Franklin and Anna Mae stood near Momma's casket, as we greeted the people who came up to view Momma's body, before the service. A few of David's friends, who probably was aware of his brawl, asked about him. Before I could say, that he was not well, Anna Mae had blurted out, "He's hungover at home!"

Franklin whispered something to her. The next time someone asked her, she had this sad look on her face, as if she was back in drama class, saying that David was under the weather. The church was already packed to capacity, as the deacons ran around placing chairs in the aisles. The ushers sat the homeless men and women that Momma used to feed, on the left side of the church and gave them each a fan. Auntie Mabeline sat on the front pew, stuck to Old Man Joe like glue, who was holding on for dear life to his red shopping bag that he refused to keep at home. Old Man Joe looked nice from the neck up. He had gotten his salt and pepper hair cut low and had his mustache and beard trimmed. His outfit? Now that was a different story.

Old Man Joe had on a dark gray ruffled tuxedo shirt, a black and white pin-striped jacket, navy blue pants and some black and white Stacey Adams shoes.

Auntie Mabeline sat next to him, looking as if she was sitting on a stack of pillows as she looked down at him affectionately. The only person missing was Rufus.

On the way over to the church, we discovered the hard way, that Old Man Joe had forgotten to take his medicine after he thought that Rufus's dangling Jerri curl were killer worms. Old Man Joe, lifted up his cane and wacked Rufus right over the head. Once we got to the church, a dizzy Rufus, got out and walked back towards the house. Anna Mae assumed that he was going to get his car and come back, but we knew better.

Auntie Mabeline whispered something to Old Man Joe, before she stood up and walked toward Momma' casket. She seemed to have calmed down from earlier this morning when we were all in the kitchen. That thought, quickly went out the window, when out of nowhere, Auntie Mabeline started screaming and crying at the same time.

"LORD, RAISE MY SISTER UP LIKE YOU DID WITH LAZARUS," she said falling over into the casket, onto Momma's chest.

Franklin ran over to get her, as he struggled to get Auntie Mabeline, who looked as if she fainted in the process, back to the pew. His strength was no match for Auntie Mabeline's oversized frame.

Two of the deacons and an usher came over the help Franklin, as Auntie Mabeline seemed as if she was coming too. The usher came and splashed some water on her face as if she was getting christened. I ran over to Auntie Mabeline and used her black peacock feathered fan and began fanning her as she sat up, laid back on the pew with her legs wide open.

"Where did Old Man Joe go?" Aunt Mabeline asked, panting, looking around the church.

At the same time, Pastor Fallback walked up to the pulpit and asked everyone to take their seat, so we can start Momma's service. That's when we spotted Old Man Joe on the other side of the church, reaching into his bag and handing out pamphlets to Momma's friends and family. We watched them take one and pass the others down. When one of the ushers approached him, Old Man Joe started speed walking around the church, as if they were in a game of cat and mouse. His ruffles, looking like they were about to swallow up his thin face.

Auntie Mabeline fell into her seat, as she rested her head on Franklin's shoulder and wailed, "I'M SO SORRY LEOLA." Apologizing for Old Man Joe's behavior, since she invited him. After about twenty minutes, the deacons and ushers were finally able to trap Old Man Joe in the back corner of the church, as a few of the ushers, went around collecting the pamphlets that he had passed out.

As the service began, Anna Mae looked around for Rufus, but he was nowhere in sight. We knew he was probably on his way to have one of his side chicks tend to his wounds from Old Man Joe's cane. Yet and still Anna Mae scoured the room with hope and denial.

Momma's service had gotten back on track until Pastor Fallback called Anna Mae up to read the obituary. Anna Mae did her normal strut up to the pulpit. She grinned and smiled sashaying by the organist who played soft music as she walked by. She smiled and waved and thanked him for coming. She walked over and gave Pastor Fallback a warm embrace, inappropriately as she normally did. But as soon as she walked to the podium, she froze like a statue.

Auntie Mabeline turned to Franklin, "Lord chile, you gonna have to get up there. That chile…" Auntie Mabeline shook her head seeming embarrassed, as she covered her eyes, holding her head down. After about two minutes, of the entire congregation watching Anna Mae look back at them with the Steve Harvey blank stare; saying nothing, Franklin finally ran up as Pastor Fallback shuffled Anna Mae off to the side, while Franklin read Momma's obituary.

Right before it was time for Auntie Mabeline to sing Momma's favorite song, "Precious Lord," Anna Mae had come over to where we were sitting; seeming to not remember her episode of stage fright.

"Oh girl, I saw Misty, Dahlia and her sister back there. They told me to tell you, hi," Anna Mae whispered.

I looked back to see that Dahlia had changed her mind about the raunchy outfit, she said she was going to wear the day we got our hair done at the salon. She had on a two-piece pin-striped jean suit, similar to the one that I had at home in my closet.

I turned back around to Auntie Mabeline, testing the mic, "Hello, hello. Can ya'll hear me?" she asked. We all shook our head "Yes."

Auntie Mabeline chuckled from the podium, as she kept an eye on Old Man Joe and then she got serious.

"Giving honor to my Lord and Savior Jesus Christ, who is the author and the finisher of my faith. To Pastor Fallback, First Lady, associate ministers, friends, and family. I bring you greetings, all the way from Savannah Georgia from the I Am the Rock Church, where Pastor Jethro Huckleberry is the Pastor," Auntie Mabeline said. She took her black laced handkerchief and dabbed the sweat beads from her forehead like a preacher.

"Oh Lord, here she goes! It's story time. She's about to put us all to sleep," Anna Mae said, rolling her eyes.

Auntie Mabeline continued, "When I heard of my sisters passing, I was very sad. Not because my sister had died but because I knew that she had left us behind, to question our faith and ask God, why her? You see, when I cry, I don't cry for my sister because she knew the Lord," Auntie Mabeline said. The folks in the congregation in agreement with her, yelled out, "Amen." She continued, "Some of ya'll don't know just how much she was suffering, with the pain that racked her body because you didn't come to visit her. There were times that she couldn't even roll herself out of bed." Auntie Mabeline took a gulp of the water that the usher had placed on the side table for her. "When we would speak and we did two or three times a day, she would say to me, "Mabel," you know that's what she called me, she said, "Mabel, I'm not afraid to die, because I have made my peace with Jesus." She said, she was worried that these chil'ren' of hers, sitting on the first row, were gonna kill each other, not being able to deal with her loss," Auntie Mabeline said as she began to walk across the stage.

"But I said, Leola, you know I got this! If I have to come up here twice a year to keep them in line, that's what I'll do," Auntie Mabeline said wiping her mouth.

Anna Mae, seeming pissed off by Auntie Mabeline's comment, said, "I'm grown and live on my own, so I know she ain't talking about me," Anna Mae said, giving me the side eye. "When is she gonna get to the song?" Anna Mae asked.

The organist kept playing the music softly as Auntie Mabeline continued to speak. "We discussed all of this, you know, way before she had that very suspicious fall in the bathroom," Auntie Mabeline commented. It was almost as if she was questioning the events that led up to Momma's fall that day. She kept going. "I said to my sister, Leola, you go on and take the masters hand. God got you!" Auntie Mabeline said as she stood straight up, arching her back. "So, I'm going to sing my sister's favorite song, "Precious Lord."

There wasn't a dry eye in the church. Auntie Mabeline sang Momma's song with so much anointing and conviction. The ushers ran around the church catching some of the people that fell out under the anointing of Auntie Mabeline's gifted voice. All you could hear was people hollering and thanking Jesus.

Anna Mae was sobbing uncontrollably, while Auntie Mabeline sang and had moved over to Franklin; she wept on his lapel.

After the service was over, the head of the deaconess board, Deaconess Franzine, came up to Auntie Mabeline. Aside from complimenting her on the beautiful solo she sang, she shared with Auntie Mabeline, that for the repast, they had prepared a table downstairs for Momma's family, decorated in Momma's favorite color; peach.

Before Auntie Mabeline could ask for the menu, Deaconess Franzine, rambled off all of the food that they had cooked. I heard her say, two roasted shoulder lambs, three whole turkeys, four pans of macaroni and cheese, a huge pot of collard greens with smoked turkey wings, four pans of candied yams, homemade dressing, lima beans, cabbage, an assortment of cakes from German chocolate, to red velvet and four pans of buttered cornbread. I heard Auntie Mabeline say that we made the twelve pies that Franklin put in the kitchen.

Auntie Mabeline gave Deaconess Franzine a hug; squeezed her tightly and said, "Appreciate ya!"

CHAPTER 34

It was 7:15 pm, by the time the limousine dropped us back at Momma's house. Auntie Mabeline asked one of the deacons to drop Old Man Joe back home after she discovered, that Old Man Joe, disrespected Momma at her funeral, handing out Jehovah Witness tracks. None of us had any idea that Old Man Joe had been studying for the past year to be a witness, until the usher told Auntie Mabeline that Old Man Joe had knocked on her door, holding that same bright red shopping bag. When she peeked out of her window, refusing to open the door, he dropped a track in her mailbox.

Me, Anna Mae and Franklin carried all of the leftover food into the kitchen and sat it on the counter. To our surprise, David was up, sitting at the table, eating a bowl of cereal.

"What do we have here?" Anna Mae asked.

"Don't start with me," David said.

Auntie Mabeline, limped into the kitchen.

"What happened to you?" David asked Auntie Mabeline.

"My corns are hurting, chile." She pulled out the chair and sat down.

"I'm tired as heck but I need to have a heart to heart with ya'll kids," Auntie Mabeline said.

"I ain't got time for this," Anna Mae said annoyed. She had enough of Auntie Mabeline. "Rufus is on his way to pick me up."

"Chile, come sit your wide behind down at this table," Auntie Mabeline said. Me and Franklin pulled out a chair and sat down too.

Auntie Mabeline looked at David, "Chile, I don't know what is going on with you but these last few days that I've been here, I've seen this kitchen more than I've seen you. I don't know why you keep playing these disappearing acts, walking around here like you are mad at the world. But the world does not owe you anything." Auntie Mabeline looked over at me and said, "Every time I ask this chile, where are you at?" She looks at me and just shrugs her shoulders. You leaving this chile up here, not even telling anybody where you going. Anybody could be watching you and come up in here and hurt this chile."

It was as if Auntie Mabeline felt in her spirit, that things in our house were not as it seemed. What she had just said to David, stirred up the anger that I felt the day I was violated. The day that David left the door opened. David looked angry, as he sat hunched over in the chair, still looking hungover.

"I told your Momma, you and Gracie can come down to Georgia and live with me but I'm gonna tell you right now, I will bust you over the head with a frying pan if I have to," she said.

David sucked his teeth.

"Georgia is too slow for me and I ain't going there!" David snapped.

"Chile, you are trying to act grown and you are not. Grown folks live on their own and take care of themselves," she said.

"Yup! Tell it, Auntie," Anna Mae said proudly.

"Chile, I have had enough out of you," Auntie Mabeline turned her attention to Anna Mae. "You walking around here like your mess don't stank. Always trying to tell someone what to do, like you are their second Momma. Take this piece of advice, drop that zero, that you married, go find you a hero and have some chil'ren' of your own!"

Anna Mae got real mad. She jumped up and started fixing her plates to go.

Franklin, chimed in, just like the peacemaker he'd been growing up. "Auntie, I don't think it will be necessary for you to take David and Grace in," Franklin said, "…with so much going on the past few months, I hadn't mentioned that my tour of duty with the Army ends in five months."

"Chile, what are you saying?" Auntie Mabeline asked.

"I'm saying that I will have served the time, that I had committed to the Army and I will be able to come live here with Grace and David. So, we won't have to sell Momma's house and I will be able to see what's going on," Franklin said looking at David.

"Thank you, Jesus!" Auntie Mabeline exclaimed.

I was so happy that I could jump up and down, but I didn't.

"When is that going to be?" I asked with excitement.

"I don't know the date yet, but I'll let you know when I know, lil' sis," Franklin said and smiled at me.

"Good!" Anna Mae exclaimed. "That means that I don't need to move back here."

Auntie Mabeline looked at Anna Mae and motioned her to zip her lips.

It suddenly dawned on me that, I probably should tell them that I was expecting a baby, before April!

CHAPTER 35

———

Five months had gone by since Momma's funeral.

Auntie Mabeline had called me every day since she left, to get an update on everything and everybody, including Old Man Joe. She also would ask me if I could send her some more ribs from Roxie's and how her old lady gang was still raving about the delicious ribs that she took back and cooked for them.

Old Man Joe was now taking the Dial-A-Bat bus; the bus that drove the elderly people in the city to their doctors' appointments or to take them to run their errands. It seemed like once a week it would be parked out in front, waiting for Old Man Joe to come out. If there was something that stayed consistent with Old Man Joe, it was that bright red shopping bag, that he still carried around. There had been a few occasions, early Saturday mornings where the bus would be out there beeping, waiting on Old Man Joe to come out. Old Man Joe would walk out limping on his cane and head to the bus, while a woman thirty years his junior would be rushing the other way, with her head down. The last time, that I went to pick up my prenatal pills at the pharmacy, I stood behind Old Man Joe in line, as I watched him slide his Viagra prescription, into his red shopping bag. It amazed me that, Old Man Joe's at his age, was still getting it in.

I didn't share that with Auntie Mabeline, during our talks because it would break her heart. Big Tuna hadn't been back, since that day that we saw him ride by in the cop car.

Anna Mae had gone back into hiding. Since we hadn't heard from her in months, we didn't know if she heeded Auntie Mabeline's advice and headed to divorce court or if she stayed with Rufus. The fact that she didn't call the house, led me to believe that she was still with Rufus.

Not much had changed with David. He didn't feel guilty for not making it to Momma's funeral, neither did he take any of Auntie Mabeline's strict advice to get himself together. Right after Auntie Mabeline left, he moved in with that woman I'd seen him with at the mall. He got up one day, packed his bags into a duffle bag and jumped into her red convertible, as I watched them drive away, as her hair extensions flew in the wind.

Franklin called me a few times a week over the past five months. I would tell him how much I missed having him here and that I couldn't wait until he got out of the service and came back home. I was counting down; there were just three weeks until he'd walk back through the door, for good.

I was finally nine months and had come to terms with being pregnant. I vowed that I would not allow the person who sexually assaulted me to take control of my mind like he did my body. Nor would I allow him to kill my dreams; he had killed my spirit long enough.

I still hadn't shared with anyone, outside of Misty, that I was pregnant. A few times I would almost slip up when I spoke to Auntie Mabeline. On my occasional run ins with Old Man Joe at the mailbox, he would get me confused, thinking I was Anna Mae and I would play along. Lord knows I had my share of "Come to Jesus," moments watching my size 6 frame grow into a size 12. Maxi dresses and flip flops in every color had become my best friend.

Misty had been a Godsend! She helped me find Dr. Freelance, a well-known obstetrician in the city. My doctors' appointments were going well and my baby was on target for my April 1st due date. Dr. Freelance had asked me if I wanted to know the sex of my baby. I'd told him no and wanted to keep it a secret until my delivery day.

A month after Momma's funeral, after I received my last check from the bank, I called my boss and told him that I wouldn't be coming back. I didn't tell him why but I'd decided to have my baby and then after he or she is old enough for me to put in daycare, I would look for a job with a better health benefits package than I had at the bank. When I told Misty, she had suggested that I sign up for financial assistance, so I did that as well.

CHAPTER 36

It was a bright sunny day. Since I hadn't heard from Anna Mae about packing up Momma's closet, I thought I'd use my day wisely, especially seeing that I was still able to move around, with my basketball belly. I turned Whitney Houston on blast and danced around in Momma's closet. A little dizzy, I held up her clothes over my baby bump, singing to the top of my lungs:

"No matter what they take from me, they can't take away my dignity, because the greatest love of all, is happening to me, I found the greatest love of all, inside of me."

I had Whitney on repeat and before I knew it, I had most of Momma's casual clothes, all folded and packed up. I sat on the floor, in Momma's walk-in closet surrounded by big green trash bags filled with her clothes, unable to move them. The six bags looked like massive wide trees in the forest. Momma had enough clothes that she could wear a different outfit every day, for an entire year without wearing the same one twice. Part of me missed Anna Mae there to help me. It was a lot to do alone. I had been in the closet for four hours before my baby reminded me that it was time for us to eat.

After I ate, I went back into Momma's closet and sat back in the middle of the bags, but this time something caught my eye. What I was looking at, hid under Momma's formal gowns as if it magically appeared out of nowhere. I crawled on the floor, moving the long dresses back and noticed a huge safe, too big for me to pick up and too far out of my reach. The lock appeared to be hanging on but the door was ajar as if someone had pried it open, distorting the metal casing.

"What is that?" I wondered.

I crawled closer to the safe to investigate as Momma's clothes that were still hung up in the closet, slapped me all up in my head, like the strips of cloth, dangling down inside of a carwash. One of Momma's shirts that laid on the floor, starting vibrating; it was my phone. I reached under Momma's shirt and grabbed my phone. I sat down on my butt and turned the music all the way down.

"Hello," I said.

"Well, hello there," the man on the other end said.

"Who is this?" I said, "I can't hear with all that noise in the background."

"How do you not recognize your own brother's voice," Franklin said.

"Oh! Hi, Franklin!" I said beaming with joy.

"So, what are you up today?" he asked.

"I've spent most of the morning, folding and packing Momma's clothes up for Good will," I said.

"Oh good. I thought that Anna Mae was going to come help you," he said.

"I haven't seen or heard from Anna Mae, since Momma's funeral five months ago," I replied.

"What?" Franklin said in disbelief, "you are kidding me, right?"

"If I'm lying, I'm flying," I said, as we both laughed.

"Well, whatever you don't get to, just leave it for when I come and I'll do the rest," he said.

"In three weeks? Oh please! I'll be done by then," I said with a chuckle.

"So how are things going between you and David?" he asked.

"Right after ya'll were good and gone, some woman came by in a red BMW and picked David up. The was the last I've seen or heard of him," I said.

"Grace, I gotta take this call that's coming through. It's about work. I'll talk to you later, okay?" Franklin rushed off of the phone.

"Okay, bye!" I said.

I realized that I had forgotten to tell Franklin about the safe that I saw. I started to dial him back, then realized he was probably still on the work call.

I stood up to stretch and decided to sit my phone on Momma's dresser in her room so that, the next time it rang, I could find it. As I turned back to go in the closet I heard a noise coming from the direction of the living room.

"Oh, my God!" I said to myself.

I tiptoed closer to the entrance of Momma's bedroom door. I could hear a sound, that was likened to someone who was shaking a door knob.

Then I heard the door knob turning.

I could hear footsteps that sounded just like the perpetrators.

"OH, MY GOD!" I said, as I ran back into Momma's closet, sitting down behind the large filled trash bags, as I tried to cover every ounce of me, with the massive pile of clothes that were still on the floor.

My hand was shaking, as I slowly, reached my arm through the bags, to close Momma's closet door up, enough to allow me to see through the crack between the hinges.

Whoever it was, sounded as if they were ruffling through papers, looking for something.

What are they looking for? Was it him? Did he come back to kill me, knowing that the baby is due any day now? I wondered.

"Oh shoot!" I said to myself, realizing that I had put my cell phone on Momma's dresser, which was twelve feet away.

The footsteps sounded heavy, eerily similar to what the person wore who violated me. I stayed quiet as I tried to peer through the crack, trying to get a glimpse of whoever was out there.

If I screamed no one would hear me.

The footsteps came closer as if he knew exactly where I was hiding. I could only imagine what I looked like, as every piece of Momma's size 24 garments of clothing, covered my body.

"Grace. Where are you?"

Oh, my God! It was Franklin.

I whipped the clothes from over my head and chest as if I was fighting to take off a shirt that was too small.

Franklin slowly pushed the door open, as he stood there dressed in his Army fatigues.

"Oh, my God! You scared me! I should throw these clothes at you," I said. Franklin bent over, through the bags and hugged me.

"Surprise!" he said.

CHAPTER 37

I sat on the floor, with Momma's clothes hiding my belly. Franklin shared with me that the person who had called him was his commander finalizing his tour of duty with the Army. His release day was today.

"Wow! You have done a lot!" he said looking around at the bags of clothes that surrounded me.

"Well, yeah," I said tilting my head to the side, "I've been in here, going on five hours now."

"Well, lil' sis', Momma would be proud. You are truly devoted," he said, at which time, I belted out Olivia Newton's song, "Hopelessly Devoted to You," we both laughed.

"Wow! Ya'll women have a lot of clothes," Franklin said lifting up the arms of Momma's suits that still had tags on them.

"OH! I knew I had something to tell you," I said.

"What?" he asked.

"Momma has a safe, tucked under her clothes way back there," I said. "It's too heavy for me to pick up."

Franklin booted down and noticed the same thing that I had.

"Yeah but it looks like Momma wasn't the only one who knew it was there," he said, noticing the broken lock.

"Move out the way and let me pull it out," he said.

Before I could even think I stood up revealing my nine-month-old belly.

"WHAT THA? YOU LOOK LIKE YOU ATE A WATERMELON!" Franklin exclaimed.

Franklin was so shocked, that he didn't know what to say or do. He turned around a few times in disbelief, with his hands on his head, like his head was about to burst. I watched him as he walked out of the closet and back in.

"Grace, who did this to you?" he said, pacing back and forth.

It was finally time for me to tell Franklin everything. Not even the closet was willing to hold my secret any longer.

That afternoon, I sat on Momma's bed and told Franklin everything that happened, last July. I told him about how David was acting that day and how I found him in the bathroom with Momma after she fell. I told him how I was sexually assaulted that same night and how I blamed David since he foolishly left the door open. I told him about David losing his license and the woman that I saw him with at the Mall, after their shopping spree. Not to mention his episodes of coming in drunk.

Franklin looked as if he had failed as a big brother.

I assured him that me and the baby were fine and that Misty had been a life saver, all throughout my pregnancy. I told him how she helped me find a doctor a few months ago and although I'm not extremely happy because of what happened to me, that me and the baby are both healthy.

"You should ask Misty to be the baby's godmother," Franklin suggested. "I definitely have to thank her for being there for you," he remarked.

"Grace, remember that day, that I told you, that you can come to me for anything?" He asked.

"Yes," I said, holding my head down.

"Don't ever feel that you can't come to me. No matter what it is," Franklin said lifting my chin up. "Do you hear me?"

"Yes," I said.

"So, obviously, no one but you, Misty and this jerk who did this to you know that you are pregnant, huh?" he asked.

"Yes," I said. "If I had of told Anna Mae, the whole universe would have known," I smirked.

"Well, I hope once you tell Anna Mae, that she learns how to be a better sister to you," he said.

"I will not hold my breath for that," I said.

"Well, I'll have a heart to heart with her, once it's okay with you," he said, "Auntie Mabeline style" we laughed.

"So where is David now?" he asked.

I realized that I had left that part out.

"He left out of here last November, with that woman from the mall. I haven't seen or heard from him since," I said.

Franklin started to remember how flashy David had been dressing and how he stood in the kitchen that day, showing off his fresh hair cut, when he teased Auntie Mabeline about the vest.

"You know, I thought it was very odd, that out of all of the days, that David would go binge drinking, it would be the day before Momma's funeral," Franklin said. While I nodded my head in agreement, a light bulb turned on in his mind.

"This dude has been acting very weird and every time I see him, he has on a new outfit but has no job. Where could he be getting money from?" he said.

At the same time, we both looked at the safe.

CHAPTER 38

Franklin jumped up and walked into the closet, moving the huge bags to the side, to create a path straight to the safe.

"Dang! What does Momma have in this thing? A fur coat?" he said as he struggled to bring the safe out of the closet into Momma's bedroom.

"Maybe it's her costume jewelry. Momma had lots of it," I said. Franklin sat the safe on Momma's queen size bed.

"I think you should put it on a sturdy table," I suggested, "Because the middle of Momma's mattress is sinking like the Titanic."

"That's easy for you to say," Franklin half smiled but carried it into kitchen and sat it on the table.

The lock on Momma's safe had been broken. Franklin opened the safe up, as we began to go through the contents.

"What's this?" I said, picking up a picture of Momma and Daddy on their wedding day.

"Anna Mae looks just like Momma here," I said.

Franklin took out a thick large manila envelope.

"What's that?" I asked as Franklin opened it.

"Oh, this looks like a receipt book that Momma kept for the rent money she received from Old Man Joe," Franklin said. "There's something else in it."

Franklin dumped the contents of the envelope onto the table. Our eyes, opened as large as a silver dollar.

It looks like Momma had saved every penny that Old Man Joe had ever given her.

"Let's count it later," he said, as we continued to go through the safe.

Two hours had gone by. Franklin and I had gone through most of Momma's stuff. Finding a range of things from our birth certificates, our medical health records to the Mother's Day art papers that we drew in school.

"I didn't know that you had a bone marrow transplant when you were little," I said.

"Dang!" I didn't know that either, he said, looking over the mountain of medical papers that Momma saved. "Wow! You've been through a lot," I said, as I read all of the hospital stays that Franklin had as a little kid.

"Yeah, I guess I blocked it all out," Franklin said. "It's surprising to me that I made it into the army," he said. "One of my army buddies got medically discharged for that; I guess it takes a lot of you if do too much strenuous activity.

"It was probably all that praying that Momma did over you," I said, smiling.

"You right about that!" Franklin said.

One of the last things that Franklin took out was a huge white envelope, that looked as if the seal had already been broken.

"What's that?" I asked.

"Grace, you have said that over 100 times," we both giggled.

"I don't know. Let's see," he said.

The front of the envelope had the name "Michael" on it.

"Who is Michael?" I asked.

"Your guess is as good as mine," Franklin said.

Franklin reached into the envelope and pulled out all of its contents. There was a hand-written letter that was folded in half.

"What does it say?" I asked.

"Dang, Grace. Give me a chance to read it," Franklin said, as he opened the letter that read:

Peaches,

I cannot thank you enough for always being there for me, getting me unstuck like a pickle in a jar. Ever since we were little, you have not only been my best friend but my rock and my confidant. There is no one else, who I would trust to leave my son with and who would raise him as if he were your own. I know you will be hot as fire at me, for leaving him on your doorstep, especially seeing that you have two kids of your own. But you have more than me; you have a husband, who can help you. I trust that he will help you raise him into the man that we could all be proud of. I hope that when you look at him, he reminds you of me, and you don't stay too mad. I hope he don't bring no trouble or heartache your way. I pray that one day, he and his twin sister be reunited. As for their Daddy, by the time they turn eighteen, he'll probably be dead from old age. I'll leave it up to you, to tell Michael who his Daddy is, since you know exactly where to find him. If I can ask one request, please wait until he's 21.

P.S. Since he just turned two, you can change his name from Michael. If he anything like his Daddy, he won't remember!

Your best friend,
Purlie (aka Jelly)

Franklin and I looked at each other in total shock!

"OH, MY GOD! DAVID IS NOT OUR BLOOD BROTHER!" we both exclaimed at the same time.

After all these years, we found out that Momma had died with a lot of "hidden secrets" that she kept hidden behind the walls of this metal safe. Franklin and I had not only discovered that David was not our blood brother, but that Ms. Purlie, Momma's best friend, was David's mother. That was two years before Momma got pregnant with me and before Daddy died. Then Ms. Purlie vanished, without a trace. She didn't even come back to get her own son, after

Momma had me or after hearing of Daddy's murder, knowing that Momma had four little kids to raise.

"Wow! I don't know Ms. Purlie but she is trifling," I said.

Franklin, sat at the table not remembering any of this, since he spent more time in the hospital, battling sickle cell anemia than he spent at home, plus he was only four. Not only did Ms. Purlie give up David but she also gave up his twin sister, splitting them up at birth. I shared with Franklin what Misty had told us about her being adopted and strangely enough, now that we thought about it, she was the skinny version of David. They both had something else in common; those green eyes.

I looked at Franklin, remembering the day that Ms. Purlie called Momma and Momma was hot as fire at her. "Now I see why Momma was so mad, that day that I overheard her talking on the phone to Ms. Purlie. Ms. Purlie had no intentions of coming back for her kids."

"This is just really messed up," Franklin said, looking lost in his thoughts; appearing to be getting angrier by the minute.

"So, wait a minute!" I said, shuffling back through the papers, so, is Old Man Joe their father?"

"If what we are reading here is correct. I would say, "he is their Daddy," Franklin said, finding it hard to make a joke.

"Oh, my God! Then that would make Big Tuna David's half-brother," I said, feeling like I was reading from a Nancy Drew novel; solving a mystery that hit too close to home.

"So, all this time, David has been living feet away from his own father and his half-brother," I said, in disbelief.

"Yup!" Franklin said. "This is CRAZY!"

David and Big Tuna were both big-boned and shared the same body type and oddly, their love for tattoos and the Hennessy.

Franklin stood up, holding his head, as if it were spinning.

If it couldn't get any worse, Franklin went back and looked at the book of receipts. A piece of paper slid out, as he held the book up and landed on the floor.

Franklin picked it up and read it:

Give to David (Michael) when he turns 21. This money represents the rent that I have been collecting from his Daddy, ever since he was born. See the black book for details.

Signed,

Leola Johnson

Since Old Man Joe had no idea that he had fathered Ms. Purlie's twins, Momma had been saving all of the rent money that Old Man Joe had paid her, ever since David was born and decided to give it to David when he turned twenty-one. We didn't know if Momma had any idea that

Misty could possibly be David's sister but Franklin was willing to share with her, what we discovered.

"Grace, count that money that was in that envelope," he said.

I started counting the money, "There's $4,700.00 here."

"WHAT?" Franklin's eyes bugged out.

"That joker has taken that much money, in so little time," he said, "Granted, it looked like Momma wanted him to have it anyways but geez. What a slimy dog," Franklin said getting angry.

It had become clear to us, that David was well aware that he was not our blood brother and that before Momma could even tell David the truth, he had rummaged through Momma's closet and found out himself.

"Grace, I don't want to think this but I think that David was the cause of Momma's death," Franklin said, sitting back down in the chair.

I sat there thinking back to the day of Momma's fall. I remembered how David stood motionless, over Momma's body, not even flinching to ask her if she was okay. I remember hearing a short exchange, thinking it was Momma fussing at David, as she usually did. David must've confronted Momma over what he found out and pushed Momma down, causing her to hit her head on the tub. He then had been helping himself to the money, sticking around, so that none of us would be the wiser or figure out, what he had did. Not to mention, he was probably too embarrassed to attend Momma's funeral, knowing that he had been the one who sent Momma to an early grave.

All of a sudden, Franklin jumped up from the table and headed down the hallway.

"Where are you going, Franklin?" I asked waddling behind him. He was headed directly to David's room.

Franklin started ransacking David's room. He threw so much of David's belongings, up in the air, it seemed as if he was making a tossed salad.

Franklin went over to David's desk and tried to open it. One of the drawers seemed to be locked.

Franklin picked up a writing pen and shoved it into the lock until the drawer released.

"OH, MY GOD!" Franklin said in disbelief, as he looked into the drawer.

David had a drawer full of nude pictures. If this couldn't get any sicker, they were all of me. David had been secretly taking pictures of me, over the few past years, when I showered and as I slept in my nighties.

"THAT SICK BASTARD!" Franklin yelled, "DAVID WAS THE ONE WHO DID THIS TO YOU! I'M GOING TO KILL HIM! IF THE COPS DON'T CATCH HIM FIRST," he shouted, as he hit the wall.

Just as I was about to agree with Franklin that David had to have been the person who sexually assaulted me that night, I shouted, "OH NO!" as I held onto my stomach.

Franklin's pound on the wall startled me; that I had pissed in my dress.

"Oh, my God Franklin. I have to go to the bathroom," I said, trying to get my balance. I turned around, trying to get out of David's room. Suddenly, a sharp pain hit me and my dress was wet from whatever ran down and made a puddle at my ankles.

"AAAAAHHHH!" I yelled.

Franklin came running over to me. "Oh, my God Grace! Your water just broke! You're going into labor," he said guiding me into the living room and sitting me in the recliner while he called 9-11.

CHAPTER 39

———————

The EMT's wheeled me straight to the back room. The same room that Momma was wheeled into. Franklin was holding my hand telling me to breathe. As the EMT's were moving me from the stretcher into the bed, the nurse asked me questions, in between contractions.

"Who do we have here?" the nurse asked.

I was in so much pain, that I couldn't respond.

"Grace Johnson," the EMT answered.

"Are you the father?" the nurse asked looking at Franklin.

"No. I'm her real brother," Franklin said as if the nurse knew what he meant.

"Well, do you mind stepping out, so that we can check Grace and see if we are going to have a baby tonight?" she asked.

"Grace, I'll be right out here if you need me," Franklin said," just yell. I mean, just tell the nurse to get me," he said. Since, I had already been yelling the whole ride.

"Okay," I said, grimacing in pain.

Franklin leaned over and gave me a hug. "You got this Grace. Everything is going to be okay," he said.

"AHHHH!" I said as Franklin scooted out behind the curtain.

Franklin stuck his head back in, "I'm sorry," as he apologized to the nurse, "Grace, do you mind if I call Anna Mae?" he asked.

"Whatever," I said, at this point, not even caring about her judging me.

"Grace my name is going to be easy for you to remember," the nurse said.

"Okay," I said.

She chuckled, "My name is also Grace but people call me Macie."

"Oh," I said, "You look like.... AAAHHH."

"You are right, Macy Gray and don't talk, just breath," Macie said, comforting me with her warm smile; showing me how she wanted me to breath.

Dr. Freelance whipped back the curtain. "Ah, my favorite patient. Grace, how are you doing?" he asked.

In between breaths, I said, "As good as I could be, Dr. Freelance."

"Well, you are in good hands," he said, looking over at Macie.

Dr. Freelance came to the side of the bed, "I'm sure you don't remember anything that we discussed during your visits, so, I'm going to tell you, everything that I will be doing, Okay?" he asked.

"Yes," I said, as I kept breathing just like Macie showed me.

"I'm going to check to see if your baby is ready to hatch," he said, trying to make me laugh, as he walked to the foot of the bed and sat on the stool.

Macie helped Dr. Freelance put my feet into the stirrups.

"Scoot down, just a little toward me, Grace," he said.

I scooted my heavy butt down to the bottom of the bed. Although I had done this a few times in his office, it still felt weird to me.

"Ok right there," he said.

Dr. Freelance lifted up the sheet as if he was looking for buried treasure.

"Mmm.... wow....... okay......" he said, peeking his head from behind the sheet.

"Well, do you want the good news or the bad news first," he said.

Dr. Freelance, obviously had never had a baby and neither had I, but I wished at this moment, he would put all of his jokes to the side and just be up front with me.

"Just tell me," I said, getting frustrated with the sporadic pain.

"Well, I'll give you the good news first," he said. "You are in active labor, which means that you have dilated to 6 centimeters. The bad news is that we need your cervix fully dilated to 10 centimeters," he said.

For some reason that all sounded good to me.

"Okay," I said.

"I'll be back. Until then, Macie will take good care of you," he said as he patted the bottom of the bed.

"Thank you," I said.

I had dozed off to sleep and woke up an hour later.

"Hi, sleepy head," Macie said.

"What time is it?" I said. It's 6:15pm. You've only been sleep for an hour," she said, "That epidural helped relaxed you a bit."

"The shot, right?" I said, feeling groggy.

"Yes," Macie laughed. "That's what was inside of the needle that was inserted in your back. It helps to relieve the pain,"

"Is my brother still here?" I asked.

"Yes. He's out there with a woman, who seems to be cussing him out. Is that his wife?" she asked.

"No. That's just my bossy sister. My brother was going to call her to tell her that I was pregnant, but I knew she would run up here, to come see for herself," I said, sounding somber.

"Grace, she didn't know that you were pregnant?" Macie asked, sounding concerned.

"No. It wasn't exactly a planned pregnancy," I said.

"Oh, I'm so sorry!" Macie exclaimed.

"Is the father around?" she asked.

"Well, let's just say, he was more around than I knew," I said.

"Oh?" Macie said, looking puzzled.

"AAAAHHHHH!" I screamed from the sharp contraction that caught me off guard.

"Okay, let's go back to more breathing," Macie said, as she did her best to make me feel comfortable, just as Dr. Freelance had come back to check on me. He and Macie placed my feet back into the stirrups.

"So, let's see how we are doing now," he said, as he rolled himself right between my legs, lifting up the sheet.

All of a sudden, he looked at Macie and whispered, "Is the room ready? She's 9 centimeters dilated. This baby is coming!"

He slid back from the chair, "I guess I took too long to come back and check on ya," he said with a smirk. "…you will be holding your baby in less than 1/2 hour," he said. I watched Macie and two other nurses rush around, preparing to roll me into the delivery room.

CHAPTER 40

Macie placed the oxygen mask over my mouth.

Just as Macie was rolling me away into the delivery room, we passed by the double doors that Franklin walked through. Out of nowhere, I heard Franklin yell, as clear as day "I'M GOING TO KILL YOU!"

I could hear a scuffle behind the double doors. I heard Anna Mae scream "NO! STOP!"

OH, MY GOD! It didn't take long, for me to figure out that Anna Mae must have called David, not realizing that neither Franklin or I wanted him here.

The scuffle sounded louder and louder. It sounded like a gang of people were fighting.

I tried to pull my oxygen mask off and Macie put it back on.

"My brother, I have to see about my brother!" I lamented.

"Grace, calm down. You are about to have a baby, who is coming any minute now. It's going to be okay," Macie said, trying to calm me down, as she looked toward the double doors, looking unnerved, in contrast to how she had been earlier.

Just as we turned the corner to enter the delivery room I heard three gunshots.

BANG! BANG! BANG!

The intercom that we passed by, blared, "CODE BLUE! CODE BLUE!"

I saw two nurses and a doctor run by us, one of them holding a walkie talkie, saying, "ONE IS DOWN!"

My heart sank! I remember Franklin saying that he was going to kill David!

I screamed, as Macie rolled me into the room and secured the door behind us. The scar from losing my mother was still so fresh. I could not bear the thought of losing my brother.

I yelled. I banged on the side of the railing. My screams muffled by the oxygen mask, "MY BROTHER! MY BROTHER!"